F. J. Stimson

Pirate gold

F. J. Stimson

Pirate gold

ISBN/EAN: 9783743301139

Manufactured in Europe, USA, Canada, Australia, Japa

Cover: Foto ©ninafisch / pixelio.de

Manufactured and distributed by brebook publishing software
(www.brebook.com)

F. J. Stimson

Pirate gold

PIRATE GOLD

BY

F. J. STIMSON
(J. S. OF DALE)

BOSTON AND NEW YORK
HOUGHTON, MIFFLIN AND COMPANY
The Riverside Press, Cambridge
1896

The Riverside Press, Cambridge, Mass., U. S. A.
Electrotyped and Printed by H. O. Houghton & Co.

CONTENTS.

PIRATE GOLD

PART ONE: DISCOVERY.

I.

It consisted of a few hundred new American eagles and a few times as many Spanish doubloons; for pirates like good broad pieces, fit to skim flat-spun across the waves, or play pitch-and-toss with for men's lives or women's loves; they give five-dollar pieces or thin British guineas to the boy who brings them drink, and silver to their bootblacks, priests, or beggars.

It was contained — the gold — in an old canvas bag, a little rotten and very brown and mouldy, but tied at the neck by a piece of stout and tarnished braid of gold. It had no name or card upon it nor letters on its side, and it lay for nearly thirty years high on a shelf, in an old chest, behind three tiers of tins of papers, in the deepest corner of the vault of the old building of the Old Colony Bank.

Yet this money was passed to no one's credit on the bank's books, nor was it carried as part of the bank's reserve. When the old concern took out its national charter, in 1863, it did not venture or did not remember to claim this specie as part of the reality behind its greenback circulation. It was never merged in other funds, nor converted, nor put at interest. The bag lay there intact, with one brown stain of blood upon it, where Romolo de Soto had grasped it while a cutlass gash was fresh across his hand. And so it was carried, in specie, in its original package: "Four hundred and twenty-three American eagles, and fifteen hundred and fifty-six Spanish doubloons; deposited by —— De Soto, June twenty-fourth, eighteen hundred and twenty-nine; *for the benefit of whom it may concern.*"

And it concerned very much two people with whom our narration has to do, — one, James McMurtagh, our hero; the other, Mr. James Bowdoin, then called Mr. James, member of the firm of James Bowdoin's Sons. For De Soto, having escaped with his neck, took good pains never to call for his money.

II.

A very real pirate was De Soto. None of your Captain Kidds, who make one voyage or so before they are hanged, and even then find time to bury kegs of gold in every marshy and uncomfortable spot from Maine to Florida. No, no. De Soto had better uses for his gold than that. Commonly he traveled with it; and thus he even brought it to Boston with him on that unlucky voyage in 1829, when Mr. James Bowdoin was kind enough to take charge of it for him. One wonders what he meant to do with a bag of gold in Boston in 1829.

This happened on Thursday, the 24th of June. It was the day after Mr. James Bowdoin's (or Mr. James's, as Jamie McMurtagh and others in the bank always called him; it was his father who was properly Mr. James Bowdoin, and his grandfather who was Mr. Bowdoin) — after Mr. James's Commencement Day; and it was the day after Mr. James's engagement as junior clerk in the counting-room; and it was the day after Mr. James's engagement to be married; and it was the day but one after Mr. James's class's supper at

Mr. Porter's tavern in North Cambridge. Ah, they did things quickly in those days; *ils savoient vivre.*

They had made him a Bachelor of Arts, and a Master of Arts he had made himself by paying for that dignity, and all this while the class punch was fresher in his memory than Latin quantities; for these parchment honors were a bit overwhelming to one who had gone through his college course *non clam, sed vi et precario*, as his tutor courteously phrased it. And then he had gotten out of his college gown into a beautiful blue frock coat and white duck trousers, and driven into town and sought for other favors, more of flesh and blood, carried his other degree with a rush — and Miss Abigail Dowse off to drive with him. And that evening Mr. James Bowdoin had said to him, "James!"

"Yes, sir," said Mr. James.

"Now you 've had your four years at college, and I think it 's time you should be learning something."

"Yes, sir," said Mr. James.

"So I wish you to come down to the counting-room at nine o'clock and sort the letters."

"Yes, sir," said Mr. James.

Mr. James Bowdoin looked at him suspiciously over his spectacles. "At eight o'clock; do you hear?"

"I hear, sir," said Mr. James.

Mr. James Bowdoin lost his temper at once. "Oh, you do, do you?" said he. "You don't want to go to Paris, to Rome, — to make the grand tour like a gentleman, in short, as I did long before I was your age?"

"No, sir," said Mr. James.

"Then, sir, by gad," said Mr. James Bowdoin, "you may come down at half past seven — and — and — sweep out the office!"

III.

So it happened that Mr. James was in the counting-room that day; but that he happened also to be alone requires further explanation. Two glasses of the old Governor Bowdoin white port had been left untasted on the dinner-table the night before, — the one, that meant for Mr. James Bowdoin, who had himself swept out of the room as he made that last remark about sweeping out the office; the other, that of his son, Mr. James, who had

instantly gone out by the other door, and be-
taken himself for sympathy to the home of
Miss Abigail Dowse, which stood on Fort
Hill, close by, where the sea breezes blew
fresh through the white June roses, and Mr.
James found her walking in the garden path.

"You must tell him," said Miss Dowse,
when Mr. James had recounted his late conversation to her, after such preliminary cere-
monies as were proper — under the circum-
stances.

So Mr. James walked down to the head of
India Wharf the next morning, determined to
make a clean breast of his engagement. The
ocean air came straight in from the clear, blue
bay, spice-laden as it swept along the great
rows of warehouses, and a big white ship, top-
gallant sails still set, came bulging up the
harbor, not sixty minutes from deep water.
Mr. James found McMurtagh already in the
office and the mail well sorted, but he insisted
on McMurtagh finding him a broom, and,
wielding that implement on the second pair of
stairs (for the counting-room of James Bowdoin's Sons was really a loft, two flights up in
the old granite building), was discovered there

shortly after by Mr. James Bowdoin. The staircase had not been swept in some years, and the young man's father made his way up through a cloud of aromatic dust that Mr. James had raised. He could with difficulty see the door of his counting-room. This slammed behind him as he entered; and a few seconds after, Mr. James received a summons through McMurtagh that Mr. James Bowdoin wished to see him.

"An' don't ye mind if Mr. James Bowdoin is a bit sharp-set the morn," said Jamie Mc-Murtagh.

Mr. James nodded; then he went in to his father.

"So, sir, it was you kicking up that devil of a dust outside there, was it?"

"Yes, sir," says Mr. James. (I have this story from McMurtagh.) "You told me to sweep out the counting-room."

"Precisely so, sir. I am glad your memory is better than your intelligence. I told you to sweep *it out*, and not all outdoors in."

Mr. James bowed, and wondered how he was to speak of Miss Dowse at this moment. The old gentleman chuckled for some minutes;

then he said, "And now, James, it's time you got married."

Mr. James started. "I — I only graduated yesterday, sir," says he.

"Well, sir," answers the old gentleman testily, "you may consider yourself devilish lucky that you weren't married before! I have got a house for you" —

"Perhaps, sir, you have even got me a wife?"

"Of course I have; and a devilish fine girl she is, too, I can tell you!"

"But, sir," says Mr. James, "I — I have made other arrangements."

"The devil you have! Then damme, sir, not a house shall you have from me, — not a house, sir, not a shingle, — nor the girl, either, by gad! I 'll — I 'll" —

"Perhaps, sir," says Mr. James, "you 'll wait and marry her yourself?"

"Perhaps I will, sir; and if I do, what of it? Older men than I have married, I take it! Insolent young dog!"

"May I tell my mother, sir?"

Now, Mrs. James Bowdoin was an august person; and here McMurtagh's anxiety led him to interfere at any cost. An ill-favored, slight man was he, stooping of habit; and he came in rubbing his hands and looking anxiously, one eye on the father, the other on the son, as his oddly protuberant eyes almost enabled him to do.

"There is a ship coming up the harbor, sir, full-laden, and I think she flies the signal of James Bowdoin's Sons."

"Damn James Bowdoin's Sons, sir!" says Mr. James Bowdoin. "And as for you, sir, not a stick or shingle shall you have" —

"If you 'll only take the girl, you 're welcome to the house, sir," says Mr. James.

"Oh, I am, am I? Then, by gad, sir, I 'll take both houses, and Sam Dowse's daughter 'll live in one, and your mother and I in the other!"

"Sam Dowse's daughter?"

"Yes, sir, Miss Abby Dowse. Have you any objections?"

"Why, she — she 's the other arrangement," says Mr. James.

"Oh, she is, is she?"

Mr. James Bowdoin hesitated a moment, as if in search of some withering reply, but failed to find it.

"Humph! I thought it was time you came
to your senses. Now, here's the keys, d'ye
see? And the house was old Judge Aller-
ton's; it's too large for his daughter, and,
now that you'll marry the girl I've got for
you, I'll let you have it."

"I shall marry what girl I like," says Mr.
James; "and as for the house, damme if I'll
take it, — not a stick, sir, not a shingle!"

Mr. James Bowdoin looked at his son for
one moment, speechless; then he slammed out
of the room. Mr. James put his foot on the
desk and whistled. McMurtagh rubbed his
hands.

IV.

The office in which Mr. James found himself was a small, square, sunny corner room
with four windows, in the third story of the
upper angle of the long block of granite warehouses that lined the wharf. Below him was
the then principal commercial street of the
city, full of bustle, noisy with drays; at the
side was the slip of the dock itself, with its
warm, green, swaying water, upon which a
jostled crowd of various craft was rocking

sleepily in the summer morning. The floor
of the room was bare. Between the windows,
on one side, was an open, empty stove; on the
other were two high desks, with stools. An
eight-day clock ticked comfortably upon the
wall, and on either side of it were two pictures,
wood-cuts, eked out with rude splashes of red
and blue by some primitive process of litho-
graphy: the one represented the "Take of a
Right Whale in Behring's Sea by the Good
Adventure Barque out of New Bedford;" the
other, the "Landing of H. M. Troops in Boston, His Majesty's Province of Massachusetts
Bay in New England, 1766." In the latter
picture, the vanes on the town steeples and
the ships in the bay were represented very
big, and the town itself very small; and the
dull black and white of the wood-cut was re-
lieved by one long stream of red, which was
H. M. troops landing and marching up the
Long Wharf, and by several splotches of the
same, where the troops were standing, drawn
up in line, upon each frigate, and waiting to
be ferried.

A quiet little place the office would have
seemed to us; and yet there was not a sea on

earth, probably, that did not bear its bound-
ing ship sent out from that small office. And
if it was still, in there, it had a cosmopolitan,
aromatic smell; for every strange letter or
foreign sample with which the place was lit-
tered bespoke the business of the bright, blue
world outside. From the street below came
noise enough, and loud voices of sailors and
shipmen in many a foreign tongue. For in
those days we had freedom of the sea and deal-
ings with the world, and had not yet been
taught to cabin all our energies within the
spindle-rooms of cotton-mills. As Mr. James
looked out of the window he saw a full-rigged
ship, whose generous lines and clipper rig bespoke the long-voyage liner, warping slowly
up toward the dock, her fair white lower sails,
still wet from the sea, hanging at the yards,
the stiff salt sparkling in the sunlight.

Mr. James Bowdoin was already standing
at the pier-head (for it was indeed their ship
of which McMurtagh had been speaking), and
Mr. James made bold to turn the key upon
the counting-room and go to join his father.
Here he was standing, side by side with him,
swaying his body, with his thumbs in his

waistcoat pocket, in some unconscious imitation of ownership, when his father caught sight of him and ordered him sharply back. "Yes, sir," said Mr. James, and moved to the other angle of the wharf, for he had caught the word "pirates;" and now, for some reason, the ship had cast her anchor, a hundred yards outside the dock, while to it from her side a double-manned yawl was rowing. And amid the blue jackets, above a dark mass of men that seemed to be bound together by an iron chain, was some strange rippling of long yellow hair, that the young man had been first to see. Yet not quite the first, for Jamie McMurtagh was beside him.

Then word was passed rapidly down the pier how this ship of pirates had been captured, red-handed, her own captain still on board, — the good ship Alarm having seen a redness in the sky, and heard some firing in the night before; and how Captain How had put it to his crew, Would they fight or not? And they had fought, rushing in before the pirate's long-range guns could get to work, in the early dawn, and boarding; so now there was talk of prize money.

Young James Bowdoin and McMurtagh were all eyes. The boat rowed up to the slippery wharf steps; in the bow were the two ringleaders and the ship's captain, in the waist of the boat the rowers, and in the stern the rank and file of the pirates, some eight or ten ill-looking fellows chained together. (The rest of them, the captain remarked casually, had been shot or lost in the battle; and not much was said about it.)

The boat was made fast, and the two leaders got up, with Captain How. The pirate captain, as Mr. James remarked, was a splendid-looking fellow. Captain How said something to him as the boat stopped, and he looked up and caught Mr. James's eye; and Bowdoin had time to remark that it was blue and very keen to look upon. Young Bowdoin and McMurtagh were standing on the very verge of the wharf, and the crowd around had made a little space for them, as the owners of the ship; Mr. James Bowdoin was standing farther back with the captain of a file of soldiers. But the second of the pirates was a swarthy Spaniard, with as evil-flashing eyes as you would care to see. And it was he who held in his arms a little girl, almost a baby, whose long yellow hair had made that note of color in the boat.

They were marched up the steps matted with seaweed; for it was low tide, and only the barnacles made footing for them. And as the pirate captain passed young Bowdoin he said, in very good English, "You look like a gentleman," and rapidly drew from his breast, and placed in Bowdoin's hands, the bag of gold. So quickly was this done that the captain had passed and was closely surrounded by the file of soldiers before Bowdoin could reply; nor had he sought to do so, for, on looking to McMurtagh for advice, he saw him holding, and in awkward yet tender manner trying to caress and soothe, the little lady with the yellow hair. The second pirate had sought to hand her, too, to Bowdoin, but some caprice had made the little maiden shy, and she had run and buried her face in the arms of the young-old clerk.

V.

While young Bowdoin's father, with the file of soldiers, marched up State Street to a

magistrate's office, Mr. James and clerk Mc-
Murtagh retired with their spoils to the counting-room.   Here these novel consignments to
the old house of James Bowdoin's Sons were
safely deposited on the floor; and the clerk
and the young master, eased of their burdens,
but not disembarrassed, looked at one another.
The old clock ticked with unruffled compos-
ure; the bag of gold lay gaping on the wooden
floor, where young Bowdoin had untied its
mouth to see; and the little maid had climbed
upon McMurtagh's stool, and was playing
with the leaves of the big ledger familiarly,
as if pirates' maids and pirates' treasure were
entered on the debit side of every page.

"What shall I do with the money?" asked
Bowdoin.

"Count it," said McMurtagh, with a gasp,
as if the words were wrung from him by force
of habit.

"And when counted?"

"Enter it in the ledger, Mr. James," said
McMurtagh, with another gasp.

"To whose account?"

"For account — of whom it may concern."

Bowdoin began to count it, and the clock

went on ticking; one piece for each tick of the clock. He did not know many of the pieces; and McMurtagh, as they were held up to him, broke the silence only to answer arithmetically, "Doubloon, — value eight dollars two shillings, New England;" or, "Pistole, — value the half, free of agio." When they were all counted, McMurtagh opened a new page in the ledger, and a new account for the house: "June 24, 1829. To credit of Pirates, or Whom it may concern, sixteen thousand eight hundred and ninety - seven dollars."

"Pirates!" he muttered; "it's a new account for us to carry. I'll not be sorry the day we write it off."

Bowdoin, in the frivolity of youth, laughed.

"And now," said McMurtagh, "you must tie up the bag again and seal it, and I must take it up and put it in the vault of the bank."

"And the little girl?" asked Bowdoin. "We can hardly carry her upon the books."

"For the benefit of whom it may concern," said the clerk absently.

Bowdoin laughed again.

McMurtagh looked at her and gasped, but

this time silently. She had clambered down
from the stool, and was gazing with delight at
the old pictures of the ships; but, as if she
understood that she was being talked about,
she turned around and looked at them with
large round eyes.

"What is your name?" said he; and then,
"Como se llama V.?" (for we all knew a little Spanish in those days.)

"Mercedes," said the child.

"I suppose," ventured Bowdoin, "there is
some asylum " —

McMurtagh looked dubious; and the little
maid, divining that the discussion of her was
unfavorable, fell to tears, and then ran up and
dried them on McMurtagh's business waistcoat.

"You take the gold," said he dryly; "I 'll
carry the child myself."

"Where?" inquired young Bowdoin, astonished.

"Home," said McMurtagh sharply.

McMurtagh was known to have an old mother and a bedridden father (a retired drayman, run over in the service of the firm),
whom he lived with, and with some difficulty

supported. Yet little could be said against the plan, as a temporary arrangement, if they were willing to assume the burden. At all events, before Mr. James could find speech for objection, McMurtagh was off with the child in his arms, seeking to soothe her with uncouth words of endearment as he bore her carefully down the narrow stairs.

James Bowdoin laughed a little, and then grew silent. Finally, his glance falling on the yellow piles still lying on the floor, he shoveled them into the bag again and shouldered it up to the bank. There the deposit of specie was duly made, the money put in the old chest and sealed, and he learned that the pirates had been committed to stand their trial. And he and his father talked it over, and decided that the child might as well stay with McMurtagh, for the present at any rate.

But that "present" was long in passing; for the pirates were duly tried, and all but one of them found guilty, sentenced to be hanged, and duly executed on an island in the harbor. There were no sentimentalists about in those days; and their gibbets were erected in the sand of that harbor island, and their bodies swung for many days (as these same sentimentalists might now put it) near the sea they had loved so well; being a due encouragement to other pirates to leave Boston ships alone. Pity the town has not kept up those tactics with its railways!

All the common seamen were executed, that is, and Manuel Silva, the second in command, who had left the little girl with McMurtagh. The captain, it was proved, had been polite to his two lady captives: the men safely disposed of, he had placed the best cabin at their command, and had even gone so far out of his way as to head the ship toward Boston, on their behalf; promising to place them on board some fishing-smack, not too far out. Silva had not agreed to this, and it had led to something like a mutiny on the part of the crew. It was owing to this, doubtless, that they were captured. De Soto, it was known, was a married man; moreover, he was new in command, and not used to pirate ways.

However, this conduct was deemed courteous by the administration at Washington, and, feminine influence being always potent with Andrew Jackson, De Soto's sentence was commuted to imprisonment for life; and shortly after, being taken to a quiet little country prison, he made interest with the jailer and escaped. It was reported that he shipped upon an African trader; and, going down the harbor past the figure of Manuel Silva elegantly outlined against the sky, he bowed sardonically to the swaying *schema* of his ancient messmate. It excited some little comment on the African trader at the time; but the usual professional *esprit de corps* keeps sailors from asking too many questions about the intimate professional conduct of their messmates in earlier voyages.

But that is why De Soto made no draft upon the credit side of his account at the Old Colony Bank; and James Bowdoin's Sons continued to carry the deposit on their books "for the benefit of whom it may concern." And so McMurtagh, who had taken little Mercedes Silva home that day, continued to make a home for her there, his old mother and his father aiding and abetting him in the task; and he carried her young life, in addition to his other burdens, "for the benefit of whom it may concern."

"Whom it may concern" is too old a story, in such cases, ever to be thought of by the actors in them.

VI.

James McMurtagh was one of that vast majority of men who live, function, work, in their appointed way, and are never heard from, like a good digestion. This is the grand division which separates them from those who, be it for good or evil, or weakness even, will be protagonists. Countless multitudes of such men as Jamie must there be, to hold the fabric together and make possible the daring spins of you, my lords Lovelace, and you, Launcelots and Tristrams, and Miss Vivien here; who weave your paradoxical cross-purposes of tinsel evil in the sober woof of good.

No one knew, or if he knew remembered, what was Jamie's age. When he was first taken in by the house, he described himself as a "lad;" but others had not so described him, or else had taken the word as the Scotch, not for English youth, but for male humanity, — wide enough to include a sober under-clerk of

doubtful age. Jamie's father had been a drayman, in the employ of the house, as we have
said, until his middle was bisected by that
three-inch tire weighted with six puncheons of
Jamaica rum.

Jamie had been brought over from Scotland
when veritably young, — some months or so;
had then been finished in the new-fangled
American free schools, and had come up in
the counting-room, the day of the accident,
equipped to feed his broken-backed father,
with knowledge enough to be a bookkeeper,
and little enough pride to be a messenger.
Only, he had no spirit of adventure to fit him
for a supercargo, — even that brushed too
close upon the protagonist for him; and so he
stayed upon his office stool. While other
clerks went away promoted, he ticked off his
life in alternation from the counting-room to
the bank; trustworthy on that well-taught
street with any forms of other people's fortunes, only not to make his own, and even
trustworthy, as we have seen it go unques-
tioned, with this little Spanish girl.

Jamie took her home to his parents, and
for his sake they fell down and worshiped;

with them she lived.   The father had had too
much rum upon him to care much for the
things remaining in this life; after such ex-
cessive external application, who could blame
him for using it internally more than most?
The mother's marital affection, naturally, was
moderated by long practice of mixing him hot
tumblers with two lumps of sugar, and of seeing the thing administered more dear to her
spouse than the ministering angel.   But the
mother worshiped Jamie, and Jamie worshiped
the little girl; and the years went by.

It was pretty to see Jamie and his mother
and the little girl walking to church of a Sunday, and funny to hear Jamie's excuses for
it afterward.

"'T is the women bodies need it," said he
to Mr. James Bowdoin, who rallied him there-
upon.

"But surely, Jamie," said Mr. James,
"you, who have read Hume until you 've half
convinced us all to be free-thinkers, — you 'd
have your daughter as well educated as yourself?"

·"Hersel'," said Jamie, meaning *himself*, —
"hersel' may go to ta deevil if he wull; ta lit-

tle lassie sall be a lady." (Jamie's Scotch always grew more Gaelic as he got excited.) It was evident that he regarded religion as a sort of ornament of superior breeding, that Mercedes must have, though he could do without it. And Mr. James Bowdoin looked in Jamie's eye, and held his peace. In those days deference was rigidly exacted in the divers relations of life: a disrespectful word would have caused McMurtagh's quick dismissal, and the Bowdoins, father and son, would have been made miserable thereby.

"The lad must have his way with the little girl," said Mr. Bowdoin (now promoted to that title by his father's recent death).

"It seems so," said Mr. James Bowdoin (our Mr. James), who by this time had his own little girls to look after.

"Bring the poor child down to Nahant next time you come to spend the day, and give her a chance to play with the children."

VII.

James McMurtagh, with "the old man" and "the mother," lived in a curious little house on Salem Street, at the North End.

Probably they liked it because it might have been a little house in some provincial town at home. To its growing defects of neighborhood they were oblivious. It was a square two-story brick box: on the right of the entry, the parlor, never used before, but now set apart for Mercedes; behind, a larger square room, which was dining-room and kitchen combined, and where the McMurtaghs, father and son, were wont to sit in their shirt-sleeves after supper and smoke their pipes; above were four tiny bedrooms.

Within the parlor the little lady, as Jamie already called her, was given undisputed sway; and a strange transmogrification there she made. The pink shells were collected from the mantel, and piled, with others she had got, to represent a grotto, in one corner of the room; the worked samplers were thought ugly, and banished upstairs. In another corner was a sort of bower, made of bright-colored pieces of stuff the child had begged from the neighbors, and called by her the "Witch's Cave;" here little Mercedes loved to sit and tell the fortunes of her friends. These were mostly Jamie's horny-handed friends; the women neighbors took no part in all these doings, and gave it out loudly that the child was being spoiled. She went, with other boys and girls, to a small dame-school on the other side of Bowdoin Square; for Jamie would not hear of a public school. Here she learned quickly to read, write, and do a little embroidering, and gained much knowledge of human nature.

One thing that they would not allow the child was her outlandish name: Mercy she was called, — Mercy McMurtagh. Perhaps we may venture still to call her Mercedes. The child's hair and eyes were getting darker, but it was easy to see she would be a *blonde d'Espagne.* Jamie secretly believed she had a strain of noble blood, though openly he would not have granted such a thing's existence. We, with our wider racial knowledge, might have recognized points that came from Gothic Spain, — the deep eyes of starlight blue, so near to black, and hair that was a brown with dust of gold. But her feet and hands were all of Andalusia. Jamie had hardly spoken to a woman in his life, — he used to think of himself as deformed. And now this little girl was all his own!

So for a year or two the child was happy. Then came that day, never to be forgotten by her, of the visit to old Mr. Bowdoin at Nahant. They went down in a steamboat together, — two little Bowdoin girls, younger than Mercedes, a boy, Harley, and a cousin, who was Dorothea Dowse. At first Mercedes did not think much of the Bowdoin children; they wore plain dresses, alike in color, while our heroine had on every ribbon that was hers. They went down under care of Jamie McMurtagh, dismissed at the wharf by Mr. James Bowdoin, who had a stick of candy for each. Business was doing even then; but old Mr. Bowdoin was not too busy to spend a summer's day at home with the children. His favorite son, James, had married to his mind; and money came so easy in those times!

Miss Dowse was fifteen, and she called her uncle's clerk Jamie; so she elevated her look when she came to our Mercedes. She wore gloves, and satin slippers with ribbons crossed at the ankle, and silk stockings. Mercedes had no silk stockings and no gloves. Miss Dowse had rejected the proffered stick of candy, and Mercedes sought a chance to give

hers away, one end unsucked. There was
this boy in the party, — Harleston Bowdoin,
— so she made a favor of it and gave it to
him.

They were playing on the rail of the steamboat, and Jamie was sitting respectfully apart
inside. The little Bowdoin girls were suck-
ing at their candy contentedly; Mercedes was
climbing with the Bowdoin boy upon the rail,
and he called his cousin Dolly to join them.

"I can't; the sun would make my hands
so brown if I took off my gloves," said that
young lady. "Besides, it 's so common, playing with the passengers."

There was a double sting in this; for Mercedes was not just "a passenger," but of their
party. She walked into the cabin with what
dignity she could maintain, and then burst out
weeping angrily in Jamie's arms. That is,
he sought to comfort her; but she pressed him
aside rudely. "Oh, Jamie," she sobbed (she
was suffered to call him Jamie), "why did n't
you give me gloves?"

Poor Jamie scratched his head. He had
not thought of them; and that was all. He
tried to caress the child, with a clumsy tender-

ness, but she stamped her little foot. Outside, they heard the voices of the other children. Miss Dowse was talking to Master Bowdoin of sights in the harbor; but — how early is a boy sensible to a child's prettiness! — he was asking after Mercedes. It was now Miss Dolly's turn to bite her lip. "She's in the cabin, crying because she has no gloves."

Jamie felt Mercedes quiver; her sobs stopped, panting; in a moment she put her hand to her hair and went to the deck unconcernedly.

But no one ever made Mercedes cry again.

Poor Jamie went to a window where he could hear them talking. He took off his white straw hat, and rubbed his eyes with a red silk handkerchief; the tears were almost in them, too. He had wild thoughts of trying to buy gloves at Nahant. He listened to hear if his child was merry again. She was laughing loudly, and pointing out the white column of Boston Light. "That is the way to sea!" she cried. "I came in that way from sea."

The other children had crept about her, interested. Even Miss Dowse had come over, and was standing with them.

"Did your father take you to sea?"

"I was at sea in my father's ship," said Mercedes proudly.

"Ah, I didn't know Jamie McMurtagh owned a ship," said Miss Dolly. Jamie leaned closer to the window.

"Jamie McMurtagh is not my father," said Mercedes. She said it almost scornfully, and McMurtagh slunk back into the cabin.

Perhaps it was the first time he had ever cried himself. . . . He felt so sorry that he had not thought of gloves!

VIII.

When they came to the wharf, several carriages were waiting. Some were handsome equipages with silver-mounted harnesses (for nabobs then were in Nahant); others were the familiar New England carryalls. Mercedes looked for Mr. Bowdoin, hoping he had come to meet her in one of the former, but was disappointed, for that gentleman was seen running down the hill as if too late, his blue dress-coat tails streaming in the wind, his Panama hat in one hand, and a large brown-paper bag, bursting with oranges, in the other. By accident or design, as he neared the wharf, the bag did burst, and all the oranges went rolling down the road.

"Pick 'em up, children, pick 'em up!" gasped Mr. Bowdoin. "Findings keepings, you know." And he broke into a chuckle as the two smaller girls precipitated themselves upon the rolling orange-spheres as if they were footballs, and Master Harley, in his anxiety to stop one that was rolling over the wharf, tripped upon the hawser, and was grabbed by a friendly sailor just as he himself was rolling after it into the sea.

"You don't seem to care for oranges, Miss Dolly," said Mr. Bowdoin, as Miss Dowse stood haughtily aloof; and he looked then at Mercedes, who was left quite alone, yet followed Miss Dowse's example of dignity; Jamie standing behind, not beside her, hat in hand.

"Ah, Ja— Mr. McMurtagh," said Mr. Bowdoin, doffing his own. "And so this is our Miss Mercy again? Why don't you chase the oranges, my dear?"

Mercedes looked at the old gentleman a moment, then ran after the oranges.

Dolly still made excuses. "It is so hot, and I have clean gloves on."

Mr. Bowdoin cast a quick glance at the envied gloves, and then at Mercedes' brown hands. "Here, Dolly, chuck those gloves in the carriage there: they're not allowed down here. McMurtagh, I'm glad to see your Mercy has more sense. Can't stay to luncheon? Well, remember me to Mr. James!"

Ah, the marvelous power of kindliness that will give even an old merchant the perception of a woman, the tact of a diplomat! McMurtagh went back with a light heart, and Mercedes jumped with delight into the very finest of the carriages, and was given a seat ("as the greatest stranger") behind with Mr. Bowdoin, while the other three girls filled the seat in front, and Harley held the reins upon the box, a process Mr. Bowdoin affected not to see.

They drove through the little village in the train of other carriages; and Mercedes sat erect and answered artlessly to Mr. Bowdoin's questions. He asked her whether she was happy in her home, and she said she was. (In his kindness the simple-hearted old gentleman still knew no other way to make a woman tell the truth than by asking her questions!) Jamie was very good to her, she said, and grandpa most of all; grandma was cross sometimes. ("Jamie"! "grandpa"! Old Mr. Bowdoin made a mental note.) But she was very lonely: she had no children to play with.

Mr. Bowdoin's heart warmed at once. "You must come down here often, my dear!" he cried; thus again laying up a wigging from his auguster spouse. But "Jamie"! "Why don't you call your kind friend father, since you call old McMurtagh grandpa?"

The child shook her head. "He has never asked me to," she said. "Besides, he is not my father. My father wore gold trimmings and a sword."

This sounded more like De Soto than Silva. "Do you remember him?"

"Not much, sir."

"What was his name?"

The child shook her head again. "I do not know, sir. He only called me Mercedes."

Mr. Bowdoin was fain to rummage in his pocket, either for a handkerchief or for a lump of Salem "Gibraltars:" both came out together in a state of happy union. Mercedes took hers simply. Only Miss Dolly was too proud to eat candy in the carriage. The Salem Gibraltar is a hard and mouth-filling dainty; and by its administration little Ann and Jane, who had been chattering in front, were suddenly reduced to silence.

By this time they had come through to the outer cliff, and were driving on a turf road high above the sea. The old gentleman was watching the breakers far below, and Mercedes had a chance to look about her at the houses. They passed by a great hotel, and she saw many gayly dressed people on the piazza; she hoped they were going to stop there, but they drove on to a smallish house upon the very farthest point. It was not a pretentious place; but Mercedes was pleased with a fine stone terrace that was built into the very last reef of the sea, and with the pretty little lawn and the flowers.

As the children rushed into the hall, Ann and Jane struggling to keep on Mr. Bowdoin's shoulders, they were stopped by a maid, who told them Mrs. Bowdoin was taking a nap and must not be disturbed. So

they were carried through to the back ve-
randa, where Mr. Bowdoin dumped the little
girls over the railing upon a steep grass slope,
down which they rolled with shrieks of laughter that must have been most damaging to
Mrs. Bowdoin's nerves. Dolly and Mercedes
followed after; and the old gentleman settled
himself on a roomy cane chair, his feet on the
rail of the back piazza, a huge spy-glass at
his side, and the "Boston Daily Advertiser"
in his hand.

At the foot of the lawn was the cliff; and
below, a lovely little pebble beach covered with
the most wonderful shells. Never were such
shells as abounded upon that beach!—tropi-
cal, exotic varieties, such as were found no-
where else. And then—most ideal place of
all for a child—there was a fascinating rocky
island in the sea, connected by a neck of
twenty yards of pebble covered hardly at high
water; and on one side of this pebble isthmus
was the full surf of the sea, and on the other
the quiet ripple of the waters of the bay.
But such an island! All their own to colo-
nize and govern, and separated from home by
just a breadth of danger.

All good children have some pirate blood;
and I doubt if Mercedes enjoyed it more
than Ann and Jane and even haughty Dolly
did. And to the right was the wide Massachusetts Bay, and beyond it far blue moun-
tains, hazy in the southern sun. Then there
were bath-houses, and little swimming-suits
ready for each, into which the other children
quickly got, Mercedes following their example; and they waded on the quiet side; Mercedes rather timidly, the other children, who
could swim a little, boldly. Old Mr. Bowdoin (who was looking on from above) shouted
to them to know "if they had captured the
island."

"Grapes grow on the island," said Ann
and Jane.

Dolly was silent; Mercedes would have
believed any fairy tale by now. And they
started for it, Harley leading; but the tide
was too high, and at the farther end of the
little pebble isthmus the higher breakers actually came across and poured their foam into
the clear stillness. Ann and Jane were
afraid; even Dolly hesitated; as for Harley,
he was stopped by discovering a beautiful

new peg-top which had been cast up by the
sea and was rolling around upon the outer
beach.

"Discoverers must be brave!" shouted Mr.
Bowdoin from above. And Mercedes shut
her eyes and made a dash through the yard of
deeper water as the breaker on the other side
receded. She grasped the rock by the seaweed and pulled herself up to where it was
hot in the sun, and sat to look about her.
There were numerous lovely little pink shells;
and in the crevices above, some beautiful rock
crystals, pink or white. Mercedes touched
one, and found it came off easily. She put it
to her lips.

"Why, it's rock candy!" she exclaimed.

There was an explosive chuckle from the
old gentleman across the chasm, and the others swarmed across like Cabot and Pizarro
after Columbus.

"Remember, children, she's queen of the
island to-day, — she got there first!" shouted
Mr. Bowdoin, and went back to his spy-glass
and his armchair.

So that day Mercedes was queen; and her
realm a real island, bounded by the real

Atlantic, and Harley, at least, was her faithful subject. At the water's edge was great kelp, and barnacles, and jellyfish, all pink and purple; and on the summit was a little grove of juniper and savin bushes, with some wild flowers; and on the cedar branches grew most beautiful bunches of hothouse grapes. To be sure, they were tied on by a string.

"'T is grandpa 's put them there," said Dolly, of superior knowledge already in the world's ways.

"Sh! how mean to tell!" cried Harley.

"And he puts rare shells upon the beach, and tops!"

But Mercedes only thought how nice it was to have such a gentleman for grandfather; and when she got back to the little house on Salem Street she acted out all the play to an admiring audience. Jamie met her at the wharf and walked home with her. It was hot and stuffy in the city streets, but the flush of pleasure lasted well after she got home. And she told what soft linen they had had at dinner, and pink bowls to rinse their hands, and a man in a red waistcoat to wait upon them.

"Is n't she wonderful! Just like a lady born," said Jamie.

John Hughson, a neighbor, took his pipe from his mouth and nodded open-mouth assent.

"And she talks a little Spanish, and can dance!"

"It's time such little tots were in bed," said Mrs. Hughson, a large Yankee person, mother to John.

"Just one dance first, Mercy; show the lady," said old Mrs. McMurtagh.

But Mercedes was offended at being called a little tot, and pouted her lip.

"Come here, dearie," said Jamie.

She went to him; and while he held her with his left hand awkwardly, he pulled a tiny pair of gloves from his pocket. Mercedes seized them quickly, and kissed him for it.

"Well, I never! Jamie, ye'll spoil the lassie," said his mother.

But Jamie heeded not. "Now, dearie, dance that little Spanish dance for me, and you can wear the gloves next Sunday."

But Mercedes looked up at Mrs. Hughson sullenly; then broke away from Jamie's arms and ran upstairs. And the laugh was at poor Jamie's expense.

IX.

Perhaps of all divisions of humanity the most fundamental would be that into the class which demands and the class which serves. The English-speaking race, despite all its desire to "better its condition," seems able to bear enlightenment as to all this world may give its fortunate ones, and yet continue contentedly to serve. Upon the Latin races such training acts like heady wine: loath to acquire new ideas, supine in intellectual inquiry, yet give them once the virus of knowledge and no distance blocks their immediate demand. Mercedes, who was thus given a high-school education and some few of the lonely luxuries of life, passed quickly beyond the circulating libraries in her demands for more. Given through her intellect the knowledge, her nature was quick to grasp. For kingdoms may be overthrown, declarations of independence be declared, legislatures legislate equality, and still — up to this time, at least — the children of democracy be educated, in free common schools, upon much the same plan that had been adopted by some Hannah More in bygone centuries for the only class that then was educated, daughters of the gentry, young ladies who aspired to be countesses, and to do it gracefully. Mercedes learned with her writing and reading, which are but edged tools, little of the art of using them. She was taught some figuring, which she never used in life; some English history, of which she assimilated but the meaning of titles and coronets; some mental philosophy, which her common sense rejected as inanely inapposite to the life at hand; some moral philosophy, which her very soul spewed forth; a little embroidery, music, and dancing; and a competent knowledge of reading French.

When we consider what education and training her life required, the White Knight in Wonderland's collection of curiosities at his saddle-bow becomes by comparison a practical equipment.

For guides in the practical conduct of life, she had been told to read two novels, "Mansfield Park" and "Clarissa." Then there were Mrs. Susannah Rawson's tales, Miss Catherine Sedgwick's, and "The Coquette." She had further privately endeavored to read the

"Nouvelle Héloise" in French; but this bored her, and — one regrets to say — the unambitious though immoral heroine impressed her as an idiot. As a more up-to-date romance, she had acquired from a corner bookstore a lavishly pictured novel in octavo, entitled "The Ballet Girl's Revenge." She could not sew, nor wash, nor cook, nor keep house or even accounts. Not one faint notion had she of supporting herself. Domestic service she thought degrading, and she looked with a lofty scorn upon shop-girls. There were some dreadful women in a house close by; if Mercedes was conscious of their existence, it was as of women who were failures in that they played the right cards badly. She held her own pretty head the higher. For she soon discarded the ballet girl's biography. By the time she was fourteen, had made another visit to Nahant, and had once been asked to a Christmas party at the Boston house, she saw that aristocratic life could offer better things. She had an intense appreciation of the advantages so imperfectly exploited by these rich Bowdoins, her high acquaintance. And was it perhaps a justification of her way of education, after all, that little Harleston Bowdoin, like every male creature that she met, was fascinated, first by her face, then more by her manners, and most of all by what she said?

Miss Mercy was sent to the girls' high school, and brought up in all ways after the manner of New England. Her looks were not of New England, however; and her dresses would show an edge of trimming or a ribbon that had a Spanish color, despite all Jamie's mother's Presbyterian repression. Then, a few years after, the old drayman died; and a beautiful piano appeared in the McMurtaghs' modest lodging. Mr. James discovered that the expensive Signor Rotoli, who was instructor to his own daughters, went afterwards to give lessons to Miss Mercy. Father and son wagged their heads together at the wisdom of this step; and Mr. James was deputed a committee of one to suggest the subject to Jamie McMurtagh. Old Mr. Bowdoin had ideas of his own about educating young women above their station, but he was considerably more afraid of Jamie than was Mr. James.

The latter deemed it most politic to put the

question on a basis of expense; but this was met by Jamie's allegation of a considerable saving in the family budget caused by old McMurtagh's decease and consequent total abstinence. Mr. James was mildly incredulous that the old drayman could have drunk enough to pay for a grand piano, and Jamie grew rusty.

"Your father's stipeend is leeberal, young man, and I trust ye 've deescovered nothing wrong in my accounts."

Mr. James fled: had the familiar address been overheard by the old gentleman, Jamie's discharge had followed instantly.

McMurtagh mopped his reddened face, and tried to enjoy his victory; but the ill-natured thrust about the accuracy of the accounts embittered many a sleepless night of his in after-years.

X.

Jamie McMurtagh still continued his rather sidelong gait as he walked twice daily up State Street to the Old Colony Bank, bearing in a rusty leathern wallet anything, from nothing to a hundred thousand dollars, the

daily notes and discounts of James Bowdoin's
Sons. James Bowdoin and his father used
to watch him occasionally from the window.
There were certain pensioners, mostly unde-
serving, who knew old Mr. Bowdoin's hours
better than he did himself. It was funny to
see old McMurtagh elbow these aside as he
sidelonged up the street. There was an old
drunken longshoreman; and a wood-chopper
who never chopped wood; and a retired chore-
man discharged for cause by Mr. Bowdoin's
wife; and another shady party, suspected by
Mr. James, not without cause, of keeping in
his more prosperous moments a modest faro-
bank, — all of whom were sure enough of
their shilling could they catch old Mr. Bowdoin in the office alone. If they waylaid him
in the street, it annoyed him a little, and he
would give them only ninepence. It was cur-
rently believed by Mr. James and Jamie that
there was a combination among these gentry
not to give away the source whence they de-
rived this modest but assured income. Once
there had been Homeric strife and outcry on
the dusty wooden stairs; and Mr. James had
rushed out only in time to see the longshore-

man, in a moment of sober strength, ejecting with some violence a newcomer of appearance more needy than himself. It was suggested to Jamie by this that a similar but mutual exclusion might be effected, at least against the weaker couple of the primal four; but there was an honorable sense of property among these beggars, and they refused to fail in respect for each other's vested rights. But Jamie was most impatient of them, and would sometimes attempt to hold the counting-room by fraudulent devices, even after the old gentleman would get down town. It was after an attempt of this sort, ending in something like a row between Jamie and his master, that the two Bowdoins, father and son, stood now watching the clerk's progress up the street. A touch of sulkiness, left by his late down-putting, affected his gait, which was more crablike than usual.

"An invaluable fellow, after all," said Mr. Bowdoin; "a very Caleb."

"How Dickensy he is!" answered Mr. James, more familiar with the recent light literature just appearing.

"A perfect bookkeeper! Not an error in twenty years!"

"Do you notice he's rather looking younger?"

"'T is that little child he's adopted," said the old gentleman. "The poor fellow's got something to love. All men need that — and even a few women," he chuckled. Mr. Bowdoin was addicted to portentous cynicism against the sex, which he wholly disbelieved in.

"The little child — yes," said Mr. James, more thoughtfully. "Do you know what he wants?"

"He wants?"

"She wants, I mean. Old Jamie came halting up to me yesterday, and ventured to suggest his Mercy might be invited to the dancing-class Mrs. Bowdoin is having for the children."

"Whew!" said Mr. Bowdoin. "The old lady 'll never stand it."

"Never in the world," said Mr. James.

"Upon my word, I don't know why not, though!"

"I'm afraid she does, though!"

"I'll ask her, anyhow. And, James, if I don't get to the office to-morrow, I'll write you her answer."

"And have me tell poor Jamie," laughed Mr. James.

"Well," said Mr. Bowdoin hastily, "you can say it's my letter — I'm late at the bank" —

The old gentleman hurried off; but his prediction proved well founded. Whether Mrs. Bowdoin had noticed the effect of pretty Mercedes upon young Harley, her grandson, or whether the claims of the pirate's daughter to social equality with the descendants of Salem privateersmen were to be negatived, she promptly replied that questions of social consideration rested with her alone. Mr. Bowdoin accepted the decision with no surprise; what pretty Miss Mercy said is unknown; but Jamie actually treated his employers for some weeks with an exaggerated deference in which there was almost a touch of sarcasm.

"Poor old Jamie!" said Mr. James to his father. "How he adores the child!"

McMurtagh was not five years older than himself, — he may have been forty at this period; but his little rosy face was prematurely wrinkled, and his gait was always so odd, and he had no young friends about town, nor seemed ever to have had any youth.

Meantime Miss Mercy went on with her piano. She was graduated from the high school the next year, and then had nothing else to do. The same year, Master Harley went to college. And there occurred a thing which gave rise to much secret consultation among the Bowdoins.

For every morning, upon the appearance of Mr. James, or more usually upon the later advent of Mr. Bowdoin, old Jamie would get off his high stool, where for many minutes he had made no entries upon the books (indeed, the entries already were growing fewer every year), and come with visible determination into the main office. There, upon being asked by Mr. Bowdoin what he wanted, he would portentously clear his throat; then, on being asked a second time, he would suddenly fall to poking the fire, and finally respond with some business question, an obvious and laborious invention of the moment.

"It's either Mercy or his accounts," said Mr. James to his father.

"His accounts — are sure to be all right," said the old gentleman. "Try him on the little lady."

So the next day, to Jamie, Mr. James, just as his mouth was open about the last shipment from Bordeaux: —

"Well, what is it, Jamie? Something about Miss Mercedes?"

"It's na aboot the lassie, but I'm thinkin' young Master Harleston is aye coming to tha hoose abune his needs," said Jamie, taken off his guard, in broadest Scotch. And he mopped his face; the conflict between love and loyalty had been exhausting.

"Harley Bowdoin? Dear me!" cried Mr. James. "How far has it gone?"

"It canna go too far for the gude o' the young man," said Jamie testily. "But I was bound to tell ye, and I ha' done so."

"Does he go to your house, — Salem Street?"

Jamie nodded. "He's aye there tha Fridays."

"Dancing - class nights," muttered Mr. James. Then he remembered that Abby, his wife, had spoken of their nephew's absence. He was studying so hard, it had been said. "Thank you, Jamie. I'll see to it. Thank you very much, Jamie."

Jamie turned to go.

"Has Miss Mercy — has Miss McMurtagh encouraged him?"

Jamie turned back angrily. "She 'll forbid the lad tha hoose, an ye say so."

Mr. James seized his hat and fled precipitately, leaving Jamie glowering at the grate. On his way up the street he met his father, and took him into the old Ship tavern to have a glass of flip; and then he told the story.

Mr. Bowdoin took his hat off to rub his forehead with his old bandanna, thereby setting fluttering a pair of twenty-thousand-dollar notes he had just discounted. "Dear me! I 'll tell Harley not to go there any more. Poor old Jamie!"

"Better ship the rascal to Bordeaux," said Mr. James, picking up the notes.

"And have him lose his course in college?"

"What good did that do us? We were rusticated most of the time, as he has just been " —

"Speak for yourself, young man!" cried Mr. Bowdoin.

"Have n't I a copy of the verses you addressed to Miss Sally White when you were rusticated under Parson White at Clapboard-trees?"

An allusion to Miss White always tickled the old gentleman; and father and son parted in high good humor. Only, Mr. James thought wise to inform Mrs. Harleston Bowdoin of what had happened. And some days after, Mr. James, coming to the office, found fair Miss Mercedes in full possession. The old gentleman was visibly embarrassed. The lady was quite at her ease.

"I 've been telling this young lady she must not take to breaking hearts so soon," he explained. "Have n't I, my dear?"

"Yes, sir," said Miss Mercedes demurely.

"And he does n't know his own mind — and he has n't been to see her for — how long was it, Mercy?"

"A week, sir."

"For a week. And she 'll not see him again — not until " —

"Not at all, if it 's displeasing to you, sir."

"Displeasing to me? Dear me! you 're a nice girl, I 'm sure. Was n't it fair and square in the child to come down here? I wonder you were n't afraid!"

"I'm not afraid of anything, Mr. Bow-doin!"

"Dear me! not afraid of anything!" Mr. Bowdoin chuckled. "Now I'm afraid of Mrs. Harleston Bowdoin! Do you mean to say you'd walk into — into a bank all alone?"

"Yes, sir, if I had business there."

"Business! here's business for you!" and the old gentleman, still chuckling, scratched off a check. "Here, take this up to the Old Colony Bank, — you know, where your father goes every day, — and if you'll dare go in and present it for the money, it is yours! You've got some music or fal-lals to buy, I'll be bound. Does old Jamie give you an allow-ance? He ought to make a big allowance for your eyes! Now get off, my dear, before he sees you here." And Mercedes escaped, with one quick glance at Mr. James, who sank into a chair and looked at his father quizzically.

"Upon my word," said the old gentleman, rubbing his spectacles nervously, "she's a nice, well-mannered girl. I don't know why it wouldn't do."

"I guess Mrs. Harleston does," laughed Mr. James.

"We were all journeymen or countrymen a hundred years ago."

But when Mr. Harleston's mamma heard of these revolutionary sentiments she put her foot down. And Master Harley (who had conveniently been dropped a year from Harvard) was sent to learn French bookkeeping in the simpler civilization of Bordeaux.

XI.

There were friends about Miss Mercy none too sorry to witness the discomfiture of this lofty aspirant. Poor Jamie, I fear, got some cross looks for his share in the matter; and tears, which were harder still to bear. John Hughson, who was a prosperous young teamster, began to come in again, and take his pipe of an evening with Jamie. He no longer sat in his shirt-sleeves, and was in other ways much improved. Mercedes was gracious to him evenings; indeed, it was her nature to be gracious to all men. She had a way of looking straight at them with kind eyes, her lips slightly parted, her smile just showing the edges of both upper and under teeth; so that you knew not whether it was sweeter to look at her eyes or her lips, and were lost in the effort to decide. So one day Hughson felt emboldened to ask if he might bear her company to church on Sunday. And Miss Sadie, — as now they called her, for she objected to the name of Mercy, and nothing but Sadie could her friends make out of Mercedes, — Sadie, to please McMurtagh, consented.

But when the Sunday came, poor Hughson, who looked well enough in week-day clothes, became, to her quick eye, impossible in black.

"You see, Sadie, I am bright and early, to be your beau."

There is a fine directness about courtship in Hughson's class, — it puts the dots upon the *i*'s; but Sadie must have preferred them dotless, for she said, "My name is not Sadie."

"Mercy."

"Nor Mercy."

"Mer — Mercedes, then."

"Nor Mercedes alone."

"Well, Miss McMurtagh, though I 've known you from a child."

A shrug of Mercedes' pretty shoulders implied that this might be the last passport to her acquaintance as a woman. "Mr. Mc-

Murtagh is not my father. My name is Silva."

"Oho! all the Italian fruit-dealers are named Silva!"

"If you 're rude, I 'll not go to church with you," said Miss Silva demurely.

. Hughson was clumsily repentant. But the young lady would not go to the King's Chapel (where she had lately affected an interest; it was the Bowdoins' church), but led him to still older Christ Church, at the northern end of the town. Here, in those ante-Episcopalian days, were scarce a dozen worshipers; and you might have a square, dock-like pew all to yourself, turn your back upon the minister, and gaze upon the painted angels blowing gilded trumpets in the gallery.

It must be confessed that Hughson had little conversation; and as they walked back, through Hanover Street, among crowds of young women, none so neatly dressed as she, and men less respectable than honest Hughson, Mercedes was conscious of a void within her life. In the afternoon she shut herself in her room and had a crying spell; at least so Jamie feared, as he tiptoed by her door, in apprehension of her sobs. Her piano had grown silent of late. What use was a piano among such as Hughson? So Jamie and the rising teamster sat in the kitchen and discussed the situation over pipes.

"The poor child ought to have some company," said Jamie.

Hughson felt this a reflection upon him, and answered but with harder puffs. "What she wants," said he at last, "is society. A good nice dancing-party, now?"

Jamie shook his head. "We've no acquaintance among gay people."

"Gay people?" Hughson elevated his brow. The phrase, with him, was synonymous with impropriety. "No; but there's my training-company ball, now; it's given in Union Street hall; gentlemen a dollar, ladies fifty cents. Each gentleman can bring two ladies. Why not let me take her there?"

"I'm sure it's very kind of you, John," said Jamie. He felt a pang that he, too, could not take Mercedes to balls.

"It's not like one o' them Tremont Street balls, you know," said Hughson proudly. Secretly he thought it a very fine affair. The governor was to be there, and his aides-de-camp, in gold lace.

Mercedes went to the ball when the night came, but only stayed an hour. She knew very few of the other girls. Her dress was a yellow muslin, modestly open at the throat, and she could see them eying it. None of the other women wore low-necked gowns, but they wore more pretentious dresses, with more of ornament, and Mercedes felt they did not even know in how much better taste was she. But John Hughson was in a most impossible blue swallow-tail with brass buttons, — the sort of thing, indeed, that Webster had worn a few years before, only Hughson was not fitted for it. She suspected he had hired it for the evening, in the hope of pleasing her, for she saw that he had to bear some chaff about it from his friends. One of the colonels of the staff, with plumed hat and a sword, came and was introduced to her. In a sense she made a conquest of him, for he tried clumsily to pay his court to her, but not seriously. Nothing that yet had happened in her little life had enraged Miss Mercedes as did this. She inly vowed that some day she

would remember the man, to cut him. And
so she had Hughson take her home.

Poor Hughson felt that his evening had
been a failure, and rashly ventured on some
chances of rebuff from her as the two walked
home, — chances of which Miss Mercedes was
cruel enough to avail herself to the full. The
honest fellow was puzzled by it, for even he
knew that Mercedes' only desire in going to
the ball was to be admired, and admiration
she had had. John was too simple to make
fine discriminations in male deference, but he
judged more rightly the feminine opinion of
her looks and manners than did Miss Mercedes herself. They had thought her too fine
for them — as she had wished.

After all her democratic education, social
consideration was the one ambition that had
formed in pretty Mercedes' mind. Her desire for this was as real in the form it took
with men as in the form it took with other
women; as clear the outcome of the books
and reading given her as of the training given
any upper servant in a London suburb, pat-
terned on a lady mistress. Mercedes had no
affections; she was as careless of religion as

a Yankee boy; this desire alone she had of
self-esteem above her fellow-creatures, espe-
cially those of her own sex and age. Her
education had not gone to the point of giving
her higher enjoyment, — poetry, art, happiness of thought. Even her piano-playing was
but an adornment. She never played for her
own pleasure; and what was the use of prac-
ticing now?

This New World life has got reduced to
about three motives, like the three primary
colors; one is rather surprised that so few
can blend in so many shades of people.
Money-getting, love of self, love, — is not
that quite all? Yet poor Jamie and Mercedes, who was nearest to him, did not happen in the same division. Hughson, perhaps,
made even the third. Yet a woman who
holds herself too fine for her world will get
recognition, commonly, from it. To honest
Hughson, lying unwontedly awake and thinking of the evening's chances and mischances,
now in a hot fit, now in a cold fit, of something like to love, such a creature as Mercedes, as she lightly hung upon his arm that
evening, had never yet appeared. She was

an angel, a being apart, a fairy, — any crude simile that occurs to honest plodding men of such young girls. John took the *distrait* look for dreamy thought; her irresponsiveness for ethereal purity; her moodiness for superiority of soul. She imposed herself on him now, as she had done before on Jamie, as deserving a higher life than he could give her. This is what a man terms being in love, and then would wish, *quand même*, to drag his own life into hers!

One day, some weeks after this, Mr. James Bowdoin, on coming down to the little office on the wharf rather later than usual, went up the stairs, more than ever choky with that spicy dust that was the mummy-like odor of departed trade, and divined that the cause thereof was in the counting-room itself, whence issued sounds of much bumping and falling, as if a dozen children were playing leap-frog on the floor. Jamie McMurtagh was seated on the stool in the outer den that was called the bookkeeper's, biting his pen, with even a sourer face than usual.

"Good-morning, Jamie," said he cheerily.

"Good-morning, Mr. James." Jamie always greeted glumly, but there was a touch of tragedy in him this morning that was more than manner. James Bowdoin looked at him sharply.

"Can I — has anything " — He was interrupted by a series of tremendous poundings that issued from the counting-room within. The entrance door was closed. Young Mr. Bowdoin cocked his thumb at it. "How many children has the governor got in there to-day? "

"One, sir," grunted Jamie.

"One child? Great heavens! who makes all that noise? "

"Mr. Bowdoin do the most of it, sir," said Jamie solemnly. "I have been waiting, sir, to see him mysel' since " — Jamie looked gravely at his watch — "since the half after twal'. But he does not suffer being interrupted."

James Bowdoin threw himself on a chair and laughed. "Who is it? "

"It 'll be your Miss Abby, I 'm thinkin'."

"The imp! I stopped her week's money for losing her hat this morning, and she 's got ahead of me and come down to get it of the governor."

There was a sudden and mysterious silence in the inner room. James Bowdoin looked at Jamie, and noted again his expression. "What's the matter, Jamie? Have you anything to tell me?"

"It's for Mr. Bowdoin's private ear, Mr. James," said Jamie testily.

"Oh, ah! in that case I'll go in and see." James threw the door open. Old Mr. Bowdoin was standing, still puffing, in front of the fire, evidently quite breathless. In the corner by the window, too rapt to notice her father's entrance, sat Miss Abby, intently gazing into a round glass crystal that, with a carved ebony frame, formed one of the Oriental ornaments of the counting-room.

"I trust we are not disturbing important business, sir?" said Mr. James the younger dryly.

"Sh, sh! Abby, my dear, don't take your eyes out of it for twenty minutes, and you'll see the soldiers." And the old gentleman winked at James and Jamie, and became still purpler with laughter that was struggling to be heard.

"As for that child of mine" —

"Psst! h'sh!" and Mr. Bowdoin snapped his fingers in desperation at his uncomprehending son. "Never mind them, dear!" he cried to the child. "Only look steady; don't take your eyes out of it for twenty minutes, and you 're sure to see the armies fighting! The most marvelous idea, and all my own," he said, as he slammed the door behind him. "Crystal-gazing, for keeping children quiet, — nothing beats it!"

"I thought, sir, you were both in need of it. But Jamie here has something to say to you."

"What is it — Jamie? No more trouble about that ship Maine Lady? D—n the British collier tramps! and she as fine a clipper as ever left Bath Bay. Well, send her back in ballast; chessmen and India shawls, I suppose, as usual" —

"It 's about Mercedes, sir."

"Oh, ah!" Mr. Bowdoin's brow grew grave.

"She will not marry John Hughson, sir."

"Now, Jamie, how the devil am I to make her?"

XII.

John Hughson took his rejection rather sullenly, and Mercedes was more than ever alone in the old house. She never had had intimate companions among the young women of the neighborhood, and now they put the stigma of exclusion upon her. They envied her rejection of a serious suitor such as John. It was rumored the latter was taking to liquor, and she was blamed for it. Women often like to have others say yes to the first man who comes, and not leave old love affairs to cumber the ground. And girls, however loving to their friends, have but a cold sympathy for their sex in general.

One person profited by it, and that was old Jamie. He urged Mercedes nearly every day to alter her decision, and she seemed to like him for it. Always, now, one saw her walking with him; he became her ally against a disapproving world.

The next thing that happened was, Jamie's mother fell very ill. He had to sit with her of nights; and she would look at him fondly (she was too old and weak to speak much), as if he had been any handsome heir. Mercedes would sit with them sometimes, and then go into her parlor, where she would try to play a little, and then, as they supposed, would read. But books, before these realities of life, failed her. What she really did I hardly know. She wrote one letter to young Harleston Bowdoin, and he answered it; and then a second, which was still unanswered.

One night "the mother" spoke to Jamie of the girl: "'T is a comely lass. I suppose you 're proud you were adopting her?"

Old Jamie's face was always red as a winter apple, but his eyes blushed. "Anybody 'd 'a' done that, mither, — such a lady as she is!"

"What 'll ye be doin' of her after I 'm gone? The pirate father 'll come a-claimin' of her."

Jamie looked as if the pirate captain then might meet his match.

"Jamie, my son — have ye never thought o' marryin' her your own sel'? I 'd like to see you with a wife before I go."

There was no doubt that Jamie was blushing now.

"Do ye no love the lass enough?"

"I"—Jamie stopped himself. "I am too old, mither, and—and too queer."

"Too old! too queer! There's not a better son than my Jamie in all the town. I'd like to see a better, braver boy make claim! And if you seem old, it's through tending of your old forbears. Whatever would the lassie want, indeed!"

"Good heavens! I've never asked her, mither," said Jamie.

The old woman looked fondly at her boy. "Ask her, then, Jamie; ask her, and give her the chance. She's a daft creature, but bonny; and you love her, I see."

Jamie pinched up his rosy features and squirmed upon his chair. "Can I do anything for ye, mither? Then I think I'll go out and take a bit o' pipe in the streets with John Hughson."

"John Hughson, indeed!" snorted the old woman, and set her face to the wall.

But Jamie did not go near John Hughson. He rambled alone about the city streets, and it was late at night before he came back. Late as it was, there was a light behind Mercedes' window-shade, and he walked across the street and watched it, until a policeman, coming by, stopped and asked him who he was. — But the virus took possession of him and spread.

The Bowdoins, father and son, noted that their old clerk's dress was sprucer. He was more than ever seen with Miss Mercedes, and she seemed to like him better than before. Women who are to all men fascinating must have a subtle instinct for perceiving it, a half-conscious liking for it. Else why do not they stop it sooner?

But Jamie had never admitted it to himself. Perhaps because he loved her better than himself. He judged his own pretensions solely from her interest. Marriages were fewer did all men so.

Still a year went by, and no other man seemed near Mercedes. Then the old mother died. To Mercedes, life seemed always going into mourning for elderly people. They went on living, she and Jamie, as before. He had got to be so completely accepted as her adoptive father that to no one, not even the Bowdoins, had the situation raised a question; to

Mercedes least of all. With such natures as
hers, there also goes instinctive knowledge of
how far male natures, most widely different,
may be trusted. But Jamie had thought it
over many times.

Until one morning, James Bowdoin and his
father, coming to the counting-room, found
Jamie with a face of circumstance. He had
on his newest clothes; his boots were pol-
ished; and his hair, already somewhat gray,
was carefully brushed.

"What is it, Jamie? Have you come for
a vacation?" said Mr. Bowdoin.

"Vacation!" sniffed Jamie. Once, many
years before, he had been given a week off,
and had gone to Nantasket; but his principal
diversion had been to take the morning steamboat thence to the city, and gaze into the
office windows from the wharf.

"It is something about pretty Miss Sadie,
I'll be bound."

"You are always right, sir," said Jamie
quietly. His eyes were very bright; he was
almost young-looking; and his manner had a
certain dignity. "And I beg you, sir, for
leave to ask your judgment."

Mr. Bowdoin motioned Jamie to a chair. And it marked his curious sense that he was treating as man to man that for the first and only time within that office Jamie took it.

"Mercedes." Jamie lingered lovingly over the name. "I have tried my best, sir. I have made her — nay, she was one — like a lady. You would not let her marry Master Harley."

"I never" — the old gentleman interrupted. Jamie waved his hand.

"They would not, I mean, sir. She will not marry John Hughson. You are a gentleman, sir, and could tell me if I — would be taking an unfair advantage — if I asked her — to marry — me. I am sure — I love her enough."

Jamie dropped his voice quickly on the last words, so that they were inaudible to Mr. James Bowdoin, who had suddenly laughed.

Old Mr. Bowdoin turned angrily upon his son.

But Jamie's face had turned to white. He rose respectfully. "Don't say anything, sir. I have had my answer."

"Forgive me, Mr. McMurtagh," said James

Bowdoin the younger. "I'm sure she could not have a kinder husband. But"—

"Don't explain, Mr. James."

"But—after all, why not ask her?"

"Nay, nay," said Jamie, "I'll not ask the child. I would not have her make a mistake, as I see it would be."

"But, Jamie," said Mr. James kindly, "what will you do? She can hardly go on living in your home."

"Not in my home? Where else has the child a home?"

There are certain male natures that fight crying. An enemy who looks straight at you with tears in his eyes is not to be contended with. And Jamie stood there, blushing fiery red, with flashing eyes, and tears streaming down his cheeks.

"James Bowdoin, you're a d—d fool!" sputtered his irate sire. "You talk as your wife might talk. This is an affair of men. Jamie," he added very gently, "you are quite right. My boy's an ass." He put his hand on Jamie's shoulder. "You'll find some fine young fellow to marry her yet, and she'll bring you—grandchildren."

"I may — I need hardly ask you to forget this?" said Jamie timidly, and making hastily for the door.

"Of course; and she shall stay in her old home where she was bred from a child, and, d—n 'em, my grandchildren shall go to see her there " — But the door had closed.

"James Bowdoin, if my son, with his d—d snicker, were one half so good a gentleman as that old clerk, I'd trust him with — with an earl's daughter," said the old gentleman inconsequently, and violently rubbing a tingling nose.

" I think you're right, governor," said James Bowdoin. "Did you notice how spruced up and young the poor fellow was? I wish to goodness I hadn't laughed, though. He might have married the girl. Why not? How old is he?"

"Why not? Ask her. He may be forty, more or less."

"What a strange thing to have come into the old fellow's life! And we thought it would give him something to care for! I never fancied he loved her that way."

"I don't believe now he loves her so much

that way — as — as he loves her," said old Mr. Bowdoin, as if vaguely. "She is n't worth him."

"She 's really quite beautiful. I never saw a Spanish girl before with hair of gold."

"Pirate gold," said old Mr. Bowdoin.

PART TWO: ROBBERY.

I.

No plummet ever sank so deep as Jamie
sank the thoughts of those few months. No
oblivion more vast than where he buried it.
No human will so strong as that he bent upon
it, bound it down with. No sin absolved was
ever so forgotten. One wonders if Jamie, at
the day of judgment even, will remember it.
Perhaps 't will then be no more the sin he
thought it. For Jamie's nature, like that of
spiny plants, was sensitive, delicate within, as
his outer side was bent and rough; and he
fancied it, first, a selfishness; then, as his
lonely fancy got to brooding on it, an actual
sin. James Bowdoin's unlucky laugh had
taught him how it seemed to others; and was
not inordinate affection, to the manifest injury
of the object loved, a sin? Jamie felt it so;
and he had the Prayer Book's authority therefor. "Inordinate and sinful affections," —
that is the phrase; both are condemned.

But he kept it all the closer from Mercedes. It did not grow less; he had no heart to cease loving. Manlike, he was willing to face his God with the sin, but not her. He sought to change the nature of his love; perhaps, in time, succeeded. But all love has a mystic triple root; you cannot unravel the web, on earth at least. Religious, sexual, spiritual, — all are intertwined.

Jamie and Mercedes lived on in the little brick house, as he had promised. Only one thing the Bowdoins noticed: he now dressed and talked and acted like a man grown very old. His coats were different again; his manner was more eccentric than ever. His hair helped him a little, for it really grew quite white. He asked Mercedes now to call him father.

"Jamie is posing as a patriarch," said Mr. Bowdoin; he smiled, and then he sighed.

Old Mr. Bowdoin did not forget his promise to have his granddaughters call upon Mercedes. Now and then they sent her tickets for church fairs. But it takes more love than most women have for each other to give the tact, the self-abnegation, that such unequal relations, to be permanent, require. The momentary gush of sympathy that the Bowdoin girls felt, upon their grandfather's account of Sadie's loneliness, was chilled at the first haughty word Mercedes gave them. It takes an older nature, more humbled by living than is an American young lady's, to meet the poor in money without patronizing, and the proud at heart without seeming rude. So this attempted intimacy faded.

Jamie gave his life to her. His manner at the office altered: he became proud and reserved. More wonderful still, he shortened his time of attendance; not that he was inattentive while there, but he no longer observed unnecessary hours, as he had been wont to do, after the bank closed; as soon as Mr. James Bowdoin left, he would lock up the office and go himself. His life was but waiting upon Mercedes.

When he was in the office he would sit twiddling his thumbs. The pretense at bookkeeping, unreal bookkeeping, he abandoned. The last old ship, the Maine Lady, had served him in good stead for many years; he had double-entered, ledgered, and balanced her simple debits and credits like a stage procession. But now he made no fiction about the vanished business.

It was characteristic of Jamie that still he did not hanker for more money. He recognized his adopted daughter's need for sympathy, for emotions, even for love, if you will; but yet it did not occur to him that he might earn more money. His salary was ample, and out of it he had made some savings. And Mercedes had that impatience of details, that *ennui* of money matters, that even worldly women show, who care for results, not processes.

It had always been the custom of the McMurtagh family to pass the summers, like the winters, in the little house on Salem Street; but this year Jamie rented a cottage at Nantasket. He told the Bowdoins nothing of this move until they asked him about it, observing that he regularly took the boat. To Jamie it was the next thing to Nahant, which was of course out of the question. But the queer old clerk was not fitted to shine in any society, and Mercedes found it hard to make her way alone. They wandered about the beach, and occasionally to the great hotel when there was a hop, of evenings, and listened to the bands; but Mercedes' beauty was too striking and her manners were too independent to inspire quick confidence in the Nantasket matrons; while Jamie missed his pipe and shirt-sleeves after supper. He had asked, and been forbidden, to invite John Hughson down to stay. Still less would Sadie have her girl acquaintances; and all Salem Street's kindliest feelings were soured in consequence. There was an invitation from Nahant that summer, but it seemed, to Mercedes' quick sense, formal, and she would not go.

She had had her piano moved down " to the beach," at much expense; and for a week she played in the afternoons. But even this accomplishment brought her no notice. People would look at her in passing, and then, more curiously, at her foster-father: that was all. Mercedes, in her youth, could not realize how social confidence is a plant of slow growth. The young girls of the place were content with saying she " was not in their set; " the young men who desired her acquaintance must seek it surreptitiously, and this Mercedes would

not have. The people of the great hotel were
a more mixed set, and among them our couple
was much discussed. Something got to be
known of Jamie, — that he was confidential
clerk to the well-known firm of Boston's older
ship-owners, and that she was his adopted
daughter. Soon the rumor grew that he was
miserly and rich.

Poor Jamie! He thought more of all these
things than Mercedes ever supposed. What
could he do to give her friends of her own
age? What could he do to find her lovers, a
husband? McMurtagh slept not nights for
thinking on these things. John Hughson he
now saw to be impossible; Harley Bowdoin
was out of the question; but were there not
still genteel youths, clerks like himself, but
younger, some class of life for his petted little
lady? Jamie had half-thoughts of training
some nice lad to be fit for her, — Jamie earned
money amply; of training him, too, to take his
place and earn his salary. Every discontented
look in Mercedes' lovely face went to Jamie's
heartstrings.

One day, going home by the usual boat, he
saw his dear girl waiting for him on the wharf.

It always lightened Jamie's heart when she did this, and he hurried down to the gang-plank, to be among the first ashore and save her waiting. But as he stepped upon it he saw that she was talking to a gentleman. There was a little heightened color in her cheeks; she was not watching the passengers in the boat. Jamie turned aside through the crowd to walk up the road alone. He looked over his shoulder, and saw that they were following. When nearly at their cottage, he turned about irresolutely and met them. Mercedes, with a word of reproach for walking home alone (at which Jamie's old eyes opened), introduced him: "Mr. David St. Clair — my father."

"I made Miss McMurtagh's acquaintance at the Rockland House last night, — she plays so beautifully." Then Jamie remembered that he had gone out to smoke his pipe upon the piazza.

He looked at the newcomer. St. Clair was dressed expensively, in what Jamie thought the highest fashion. He wore kid gloves and a high silk hat; he had a white waistcoat and a very black mustache. Mercedes had blushed again when she presented him, and suddenly there was a burst of envy in poor Jamie's heart.

II.

No girl, before she came to love, ever scrutinized a suitor so closely as old Jamie did St. Clair. The little old Scotch clerk was quicker far to see the first blossoms of love in her heart than Mercedes herself, than any mother could have been, for each one bore a pang for him; and he, who had renounced, and then set his heart to share each feeling with her, who had wanted but her confidence, wanted but to share with her as some girl might her heart histories, now found himself far outstripping her in conscious knowledge. He did not realize the impossibility of the sympathy he dreamed. He had fondly thought his man's love a justification for that intimacy from which, in natures like Mercedes', even a mother's love is excluded.

All Jamie's judgment was against the man, and yet his heart was in touch with hers to feel its stirring for him. The one told him he was not respectable; the other that he was romantic. His career was shadowy, like his hair. In those days still a mustache bore with it some audacity, and gave a man who frankly lived outside the reputable callings something of the buccaneer. St. Clair called himself a gentleman, but did not pretend to be a clerk, and frankly avowed that he was not in trade. Jamie could not make him out at all. He hoped, indeed, he was a gentleman. Had he been in the old country, he could have credited it better; but gentlemen without visible means of support were, in those days, unusual in Boston.

Poor Jamie watched his daughter like any dowager, that summer. But the consciousness of his own sin (for so now he always thought of it) troubled him terribly. How could he urge his lady to repel the advances of this man without being open to the charge of selfishness, of jealousy? Jamie forgot that the girl had never known he loved her.

He made feeble attempts to egg on Hughson. The honest teamster was but a lukewarm lover. His point of view was that the girl looked down upon him, and this chilled his passion. He had come to own his teams

now. He never drove them. He was a cap-
italist, an employer of labor; and, at Jamie's
request, he came down one night, in black
broadcloth and red-handed, to pass the night.
But it did not work. When Mr. St. Clair
called in the evening, he adopted a tone of
treating both Jamie and Hughson as elderly
pals, so that the latter lost his temper, and, as
Mercedes claimed, insulted his elegant rival.

Then Jamie bade Hughson to come no
more, for his love for Mercedes was so true
that he felt in his heart why St. Clair ap-
pealed more to hers.

But the summer was a long and anxious
one, and he was glad when it was over and
they were back in Salem Street. They had
made no other acquaintance at Nantasket.
"Society" to Jamie remained a sealed book.
Clever Mercedes was not clever enough to see
he knew she blamed him for it. St. Clair only
laughed. "These people are nobody," said
he; and he talked of fashionable and equi-
paged friends he had known in other places.
Where? Jamie suspected, race-courses; his
stories of them bore usually an equine flavor.
But he was not a horse-dealer; his hands were
too white for that.

Poor old Mr. Bowdoin had had a hangdog feeling with old Jamie ever since that day his son had laughed. He had dared criticise nothing he noticed at the office, and Jamie grew more crusty and eccentric every day. James Bowdoin was less indulgent, and soon saw that something new was in the wind. But the last thing that both expected was a demand on Jamie's part for an increased salary. Jamie made it respectfully, with his hat off, twirling in his hand, and the Bowdoins eyed him.

" It isna that I 'm discontented with the place or the salary in the past," said Jamie, " but our expenses are increasing. I have rented a house in Worcester Square."

" In Worcester Square ? And the one in Salem Street ? "

" ' T is too small for me family needs," said Jamie. " I have sold it."

" Too small ? "

" Me daughter is about to be married," said Jamie reluctantly.

" Dear me ! " exclaimed the Bowdoins in a breath. " May we congratulate her ? "

" Ye may do as ye like," said Jamie. " 'T is one Mr. David St. Clair, — a gentleman, as he tells me."

" Is he to live with you, then ? "

" Yes, sir. He wants work — that is " — Jamie hesitated.

" He has no occupation ? "

Jamie was visibly irritated. " If I bring the gentleman down, ye may ask him your ain sel'."

" No, no," said Mr. James. " That is, we should, of course, be glad to meet the gentleman at any time. What is his name ? "

" David St. Clair."

" David Sinclair," repeated the old gentleman.

" Mercedes Silva," said Mr. James musingly.

" McMurtagh, if you please," said Jamie.

" Jamie," said old Mr. Bowdoin, " our business is going away. The steamers will ruin it. For a long time there has not been enough to occupy a man of your talents. And the old bookkeeper at the bank — the Old Colony Bank — has got to resign. I 've already asked the place for you. The salary is — more than we here can afford to pay you. In fact, we may close the counting-room."

Jamie rubbed his nose and shifted his feet.

" Ta business is a goot business, and t' firm is a fine old firm." It was evident he was in the throes of unexpressed affection. In all his life he had never learned to express it. " Ye 'll na be closing the old counting-room ? "

" I may come down here every day or so, just to keep my trusts up. I 'll use it for a writing-room ; it 's near the bank " —

" An' I 'll come down an' keep the books for you, sir," said Jamie ; and the " sir " from his lips was like a caress from another man.

III.

Jamie took his place on the high stool behind the great ledgers of the Old Colony Bank, and the house on Worcester Square was even bought, with his savings and the price of the house on Salem Street. Only one thing Jamie flatly refused, and that was to permit Mercedes' marriage until St. Clair had some visible means of support. She pouted at this and was cruel ; but for once the old clerk was inflexible, even to her. Mercedes would perhaps have married against his will, but Mr. St. Clair had his reason for submitting.

And that gentleman was particular in his choice of occupation, and Mercedes yet more particular for him. The class of which St. Clair came is a peculiar one, hardly known to the respectable world, less known then than now; and yet it has often money, kindliness, reputability even, among its members: they marry and have children among their own class; they are not church-going, but yet they are not criminal. As actor families maintain themselves for many generations (not the stars, but the ordinary histrionic families; you will find most of the names on the playbills to-day that were there in the last century, neither above nor below their old position), so there are sporting families who live in a queer, not unprosperous world of their own, marry and bring up children, and leave money and friends behind them when they die. And Sinclair came of people such as these. "St. Clair" was his own invention. Of course Jamie did not know it, nor did Mercedes; and in fact he was honestly in love with her, to the point of changing his way of life to one of routine and drudgery.

But no place could be found (save, indeed, a

retail grocer's clerkship), and Mercedes began
to grow worried, and occasionally to cry. St.
Clair spent his evenings at the house; and at
such times Jamie would wander helplessly
about the streets. St. Clair's one idea was to
be employed about the bank, to become a
banker. Had he been competent to keep the
books, I doubt not Jamie would have given
them up to him.

Great is the power of persuasion backed by
love, even in a bent old Scotchman. Will it
be believed, Jamie teased and schemed and
promoted until he made a vacancy of the place
of messenger, and got it for his son-in-law.
Perhaps old Mr. Bowdoin had ever had a
slight feeling of remorse since he had seen
nipped in the bud that affair with young
Harleston. He did not approve of the present
match. Yet he fancied the bridegroom might
be a safer spouse with a regular occupation
and a coat more threadbare than he habitually
wore.

Nothing now stood in the way of the marriage; and it took place with some *éclat*, — in
King's Chapel, indeed, with all the Bowdoins,
even to Mrs. Abby. Jamie gave the bride

away. Hughson (to Mercedes' relief) took it
a bit rusty and would not come. Then the
pair went on a wedding journey to Niagara
and Trenton Falls; and old Jamie, the day
after the ceremony, came down looking happier than he had seemed for years. There
was a light in his lonely old face; it comes
rarely to us on earth, but, by one who sees it,
it is not forgotten. Old Mr. Bowdoin saw it;
and, remembering that interview scarce two
years gone by, his nose tingled. It is rare that
natures with such happy lives as his are so
" dowered with the love of love." But when
old Jamie looked at him, he but asked some
business question ; and Jamie marveled that
the old gentleman blew his nose so hard and
damned the weather so vigorously.

When the St. Clairs came back, Jamie
moved to an upper back room, and gave them
the rest of the new house. Mercedes was de-
votedly in love with her husband. She would
have liked to meet people, if but to show him to
them. But she knew no one worthy save the
Bowdoins, and they did not get on with him.
His own social acquaintance, of which he had
boasted somewhat, appeared to be in other

cities. And *ennui* (which causes more harm
in the world than many a more evil passion)
began imperceptibly to take possession of him.

However, they continued to live on together.
St. Clair was fairly regular at his work; and
all went well for more than a year.

IV.

No year, probably, of James McMurtagh's
life had he been so happy. It delighted him
to let St. Clair away early from the bank; and
to sit alone over the ledgers, imagining St.
Clair's hurrying home, and the greeting kiss,
and the walk they got along the shells of the
beach before supper, with the setting sun
slanting to them over the wide bay from the
Brookline hills. When they took the meal
alone, it delighted Jamie to sit at Mercy's
right and have her David help him; or, when
they had " company," it pleased the old man
almost as much to stay away and think
proudly of them. Such times he would sit
alone on the Common and smoke his pipe, and
come home late and let himself in with his
latch-key, and steal up quickly to his own bedroom at the top of the house.

Now that he was so happy, and had left his old friends the Bowdoins, a wave of unconscious affection for them spread over his soul. Under pretext of keeping their accounts straight — which now hardly needed balancing even once a month — old Jamie would edge down to the counting-room upon the wharf, after hours, or even for a few minutes at noontime (perhaps sacrificing his lunch therefor), to catch old Mr. Bowdoin at his desk and chat with him (under plea of some omitted entry needing explanation), and tell him how well David was doing, and Mercedes so happy, and what company they had had to tea the night before. So that one day Mr. Bowdoin even ventured to give him a golden bracelet young Harleston Bowdoin had sent, soon after the wedding, from France; and Jamie took it without a murmur. "Ah, 't is a pity, sir, ye din't keep the old house up, for the sake of the young gentlemen, if nothing more," said he; and "Ah, Jamie," was Mr. Bowdoin's reply, "it 's all dirty coal-barges now; the old house would not know its way about in steamers. We 'll have to take to banking, like yourself and Sinclair there."

Jamie laughed with pleasure, and father and son went each to a window to watch him as he sidled up the street.

" Caroline never would have stood it," said the old man.

" Neither would Abby," said the younger one. " Yet you made me marry her ; " and they both chuckled. It was the habit of the Bowdoin males to marry them to women without a sense of humor, and then to take a mutual delight in the consequences.

" You only married her to get a house," said the old man. (This was the inexhaustible joke they shared against Mrs. Abby that in nearly twenty years had never failed to rouse her serious indignation.) " I saw her coming out of that abolitionist meeting yesterday."

" That 's cousin Wendell Phillips got her into that," said Mr. James. " Old Jamie was there, too."

" Old Jamie has got so much love to spare that it spills around," said Mr. Bowdoin, " even on comfortable niggers just decently clothed. That 's not your wife's trouble." To which the son had no other repartee than

" James ! " drawled in the solemn bass of amazed indignation that his mother's voice assumed when goaded into speech by his father's sallies. It was his boast that " Abby " never yet had ventured to address him thus. And so this precious pair separated; the father going home to his grandchildren, and the son to the club for his afternoon rubber of whist. They still took life easy in the forties.

Why was it that old Jamie, who should by rights have had his heart broken, was happier than fortunate David? Both loved the same woman; and no tenor hero ever loved so deeply as old Jamie, and he had lost her. But he came of the humble millions that build the structure of human happiness silently, by countless, uncounted little acts. David was of the ephemera, the pleasure-loving insects. Now these will settle for a time; but race will tell, and they are not the race of quiet labor.

One almost wonders, in these futureless times, that so many of the former still remain. For the profession of pleasure is so easy, so remunerative; even of money it often has no lack. St. Clair came of a family that, from horse-racing, bar-keeping, betting, had found money easier to get than ever had Jamie's people, and (when they had chosen to invest it) had invested it in less reputable but more productive ways. One fears the spelling-books mislead in their promise of instant, adequate reward and punishment. The gods do not keep a dame-school for us here on earth, and their ways are less obvious than that. One hazards the suggestion, it is fortunate if our multitudes (in these socialistic, traditionless times) do not yet discover how comfortable, for hedonistic ends, their sons and daughters still may be without respectability and reputability.

St. Clair lived before them, and his mind was never analytic. The word "bore" had not yet been imported, nor the word "ennui" naturalized in a civilization whence two hundred years of Puritans had sought to banish it. But although Adam set the example of falling to the primal woman, it may be doubted whether Eve, at least, had not a foretaste of the modern evil. And more souls go now to the devil (if they could hope there were one!) for the being bored than any other cause.

David did not know what ailed him. He loved his wife (not too exclusively : that was not in his shallow nature) ; he had a fine house and the handling of money. To his friends he was a banker. They were at first envious of his reputability, and that pleased him while it lasted. But it annoyed him that it had not dawned on their untutored minds that handling money was not synonymous with possession. A banker! At least he had the control of money; could lend it; might lend it to his friends.

There was, in those days, an outpost of Satan — overrated perhaps in importance by the college authorities, with proportionate overawing effect upon the students — on the riverside, over against Cambridge. Here "trials of speed," trotting speed, were held; bar-rooms existed; it was rumored pools were sold. Hither the four hundred, the liberal four hundred, of Boston's then existent vice, were wont to repair and witness contests for "purses." It was worth, in those days, a bank clerk's position or an undergraduate's degree ever to be seen there.

It may be imagined with what terror — a

terror even transmuting itself to pity dictating a refusal on Mercedes' part — old Jamie heard of a proposition, one holiday, that David should take his wife there. Mercedes would not go; and St. Clair laughed at her, in private, and went alone. She was forced to be the accomplice of his going.

The fact is, St. Clair, from the tip of his mustache to his patent-leather shoes, was bored with regular hours, respectability, and the assurance of an income adequate to his ordinary spending. Something must be done for joy of life. He gave a champagne supper to his old cronies, at a tavern by the wayside, and bore their chaff. Then he bet. Then he stayed away from home a day or two.

A butterfly cares but for sunshine. His love for Mercedes was quite animal; he cared nothing for her mind; all poor Jamie's expensive schooling was wasted, more unappreciated by him than it would have been by John Hughson. So, one day, St. Clair came home to find her crying; and his love for her then ended.

V.

Mercedes, remember, lived in the earlier half of this strange century, now so soon to go to judgment. In these last years, when women seek men's rights in exchange for woman's reason, reactionary males have criticised them as children swapping old lamps for new, fine instruments for coarser toys. As a poet has put it, why does

> " a woman
> Dowered by God with power of life or death
> Now cry for coarser tools,"

and seek to exchange the ballot for Prospero's wand? Like other savages, she would exchange fine gold for guns and hatchets. (Beads, trinkets, the men might pardon them!)

A woman of power once said she had rather reign than govern. But reigns, with male St. Clairs, so soon are over! Mercedes' dynasty had ended. She knew it before St. Clair was conscious of it, and poor Jamie knew it when she did.

It was his custom to stay late at the bank, after hours. It closed at two o'clock; and in

those days all merchants then went home to
their dinner.   Jamie, unknown to the cashier,
would assume what he could of St. Clair's
work, to get him home the sooner to Mercedes.
It is to be hoped he always went there.

As one looks back on the days of great
events, one wonders that the morning of them
was not consciously brightened or shadowed
by the happening to come.   For, after many
years, that morning, — of the meeting, or the
news, or whatever it was, — dull and gray as
in fact it was, seems now all glorified in memory, illumined with the radiance it bore among
its hours.   Jamie never could remember what
he did that morning or that day.   It was close
to half past four by the clock; the cashier,
the other clerks, had gone; the charwoman
was sweeping.   He was mechanically counting
over the cash in the cash drawer (it had been
counted over before by the teller, so Jamie's
count was but excess of caution); he was sep-
arating the gold and silver and Massachusetts
bills from the bills that came from banks of
other States.   (These never were credited until
collected, and so not counted yet as cash, but
credited to the collection account; in Jamie's

eyes, bank-bills of other States were not so
honest as Massachusetts issues, any more than
their merchants were like James Bowdoin's
Sons). He was thinking, with a sadness not
admitted to himself, of Mercedes; trying to
believe his judgment a fancy; trying to see, in
his mind's eye, David's arrival home (he had
sent him off the half an hour before), hoping
even for kisses by him for Mercedes (for he
grudged him not her love, but wished his the
greater). And now, with half his mind, he
was adding up the long five columns of figures,
as he could do almost unconsciously, thinking
of other things. He had carried down the
third figure, when suddenly there came that
warm stirring at the roots of the hair that
presages, to the slower brain, the heart's grasp
of a coming disaster.

The figure was a 4 he carried down. His
count of the cash had made it a 2.

Nonsense. He passed his hand to his
quickened heart and made an effort to slow
his breath. It was his mistake; he had been
thinking of other things, of Mercedes. He
leaned back against the high desk and rested.
Besides, what foolish fear to jump at fault for

error, at fault of David St. Clair! He had not been near the cash drawer.

It was the teller's mistake. And this time poor Jamie added up like a schoolboy, totting each figure. No thought of his Mercedes now.

Fourteen thousand *four* hundred and twelve, sixty-four cents. The teller's addition was right.

Jamie looked at the cash again. There were two piles of bank-bills, one of gold and silver. Among the former was one packet of hundred-dollar bills in a belt, marked "$5000." This wrapper he had not (as he now remembered) verified when he had made his count. His heart stood still; prompting the head to remember that it was a package collected by the bank's messenger on a discount, by David St. Clair.

Poor Jamie tore off the band. He sat down, and counted the bills again with a shaking hand.

There were only forty-eight of them.

VI.

The packet was two hundred dollars short.
And David had brought it in.

Two hundred dollars! Only two hundred
dollars! In God's name, why did he not borrow it, ask me for it? thought poor Jamie.
He must have known it would be at once discovered. And mixed curiously with Jamie's
dismay was a business man's contempt for the
childishness of the theft. And yet they called
such men sharpers!

For never from that moment, from that
time on, did poor Jamie doubt the sort of man
Mercedes had married. Never for one moment did the idea occur to him that the rob-
bery might be overlooked, the man reformed.
Jamie's heart was as a little child's, but his
head was hard enough. He had seen too much
of human nature, of business methods and
ways, to doubt what this thing meant or what
it led to. He had been trying to look through
Mercedes' eyes. He had known him for a
gambler all along; and now it appeared that
he was a man not to be trusted even with
money. And he had given him Mercedes!

There had been Harley Bowdoin. She had liked him first; and but for them, his employers — But no; old Jamie could not blame his benefactor, even through his wife. It was not that. No one was at fault but he himself. If he had even loved her less, it had been better for her: 't was his fault, again his fault.

Sobbing, he went through the easy form of making good the theft; this with no thought of condoning the offense, but for his little girl's name. It was simple enough: it was but the drawing a check of his own to cover the loss. Oh, the fool the scoundrel had been!

Jamie drew the check, and canceled it, and added it to the teller's slip. Then he closed the heavy books, put the cash drawer back in the safe, closed the heavy iron doors, gave a turn of his wrist and a pull to the handle, said a word to the night-watchman, and went out into the street. It was the soft, broad sunlight of a May afternoon; by the clock at the head of the street he saw that it was not yet six o'clock. But for once Jamie went straight home.

Mr. St. Clair had not come in, said the servant. (They now kept one servant.) Mrs.

St. Clair was lying down. Jamie went into the parlor, contrary to his wont, and sat down awkwardly. It was furnished quite with elegance: Mercedes had been so proud of it! His little girl! And now he had married her to a thief! People might come to scorn her, his Mercedes.

They had tea alone together; and Jamie was very tender to her, so that she became frightened at his manner, and asked if anything was wrong with David.

"No," said Jamie. "Has he not been home? Do you not know where he is?"

"No," sighed the wife. "He has always told me before this."

Jamie touched her hand shyly. "Do you still love him, dear?"

But she flung away from him angrily, and went upstairs. And old Jamie waited. He dared not smoke his pipe in the parlor, nor even on the doorstep (which was a pleasant place; there was a little park, with trees, in front), for Mercedes thought it ungenteel. The present incongruity of this regard for appearances never struck Jamie, and he waited there. After eleven o'clock he fancied he might venture; the neighbors were not likely to be up to notice it. So he lit his pipe and listened. There was still a light in her window; but David St. Clair did not come. Her window stood open, and Jamie listened hard to hear if she were crying. Shortly after midnight the birds in the square began to twitter, as if it were nearly dawn. Then they went to sleep again, but Jamie went on smoking.

It was daylight when St. Clair appeared, in a carriage. He had the look of one who has been up all night, and started nervously as he saw Jamie on the doorstep. Then he pulled himself together, buttoning his coat, and, giving the driver a bill, he turned to face the old clerk.

"Taking an early pipe, Mr. McMurtagh?"

"I know what ye ha' done," said Jamie simply. "I ha' made it guid; but ye must go."

St. Clair's bravado collapsed before Jamie's directness.

"Made what good?" he blustered.

"The two hundred dollars ye took," said Jamie.

"Two hundred dollars? I took? Old man, you 're crazy."

"I tell ye I ha' made it guid," said Jamie.

"Made it good? I could do that myself, if — if " —

"Perhaps ye 'll be having the money about ye now?" said Jamie. "Can ye give it me?"

St. Clair abandoned pretense. Perhaps curiosity overcame him, or his morning nerves were not so good as Jamie's. "Of course I 'll get the money. I lent it to a friend. But how did you ever know the d—d business was short?"

Jamie looked at him sadly. This was the man he had hoped to make a man of business. "Mon, why did n't ye ask me for it? Do ye suppose they didna count their money the nicht?"

"You 're so d—d mean!" swore St. Clair. "Have you told my wife?"

"Ye 'll not be telling Mercy?" gasped Jamie, unmindful of the result. "I have told no one."

"I 'll make it all right with the teller, then," said the other.

"Ye 'll na be going back to the bank!" cried Jamie.

"Not go back? Do you suppose I can't be

trusted with a matter of two hundred dollars?"

"Ye'll not be going back to the bank!" said Jamie firmly. "Ye'll be taking Mr. Bowdoin's money next."

"If it were n't for the teller— He's not a gentleman, and last week I was fool enough to tell him so. Did the teller find it out?"

"I found it out my own sel'."

"Then no one else knows it?"

"Ye canna go back."

"Then I'll tell Sadie it's all your fault," said David.

Poor Jamie knocked his pipe against the doorstep and sighed. The other went upstairs.

VII.

It was some days after this that old Mr. Bowdoin came down town, one morning, in a particularly good humor. To begin with, he had effected with unusual success a practical joke on his auguster spouse. Then, he had gone home the night before with a bad cold; but (having given a family dinner in celebration of his wife's birthday and the return to

Boston of his grandson Harley, and confined himself religiously to dry champagne) he had arisen quite cured.   But at the counting-room he was met by son James with a face as long as the parting glass of whiskey and water he had sent him home with at eleven the previous evening.   " James Bowdoin, at your time of life you should not take Scotch whiskey after madeira," said he.

" You seem fresh as a May morning," said Mr. James.   " Did the old lady find out about the bronze Venus ? "

Son and father chuckled.   The old gentleman had purchased in his wife's name a nearly life-size Venus of Milo in bronze, and ordered it sent to the house, with the bill unreceipted, just before the dinner; so the entire family had used their efforts to the persuading old Mrs. Bowdoin that she had acquired the article herself, while shopping, and then forgotten all about it.

" 'Mrs. J. Bowdoin, Dr. To one Bronze Venus. One Thousand Dollars. Rec'd Paym't ' — blank ! " roared Mr. Bowdoin.   " I told her she must pay it out of her separate estate, — I could n't afford such luxuries."

" ' Why, James ! ' " mimicked the younger.

" ' I never went near the store,' " mimicked the older.

" And when we told her it was all a sell, she was madder than ever."

" Your mother never could see a joke," sighed Mr. Bowdoin. " She says the statue 's improper, and she 's trying to get it exchanged for chandeliers. She would n't speak to me when I went to bed ; and I told her I 'd a bad cold on my lungs, and she 'd repent it when I was gone. But to-day she 's madder yet."

Mr. James Bowdoin looked at his father inquiringly.

Mr. Bowdoin laughed aloud. " She had n't a good night, she says."

" Dear me," said the younger man, " I 'm sorry."

" Yes. I 'd a bad cold, and I spoke very hoarsely when I went to bed. And in the night she woke up and heard a croupy sound. It was this," and Mr. Bowdoin produced a compressible rubber ball with a squeak in it. " ' James,' said she — you know how she says ' James ' ? "

Mr. James Bowdoin admitted he had heard the intonation described.

"'James,' says she, 'is that you?' I only squeaked the ball, which I had under the bed-clothes. 'James, are you ill?' 'It's my chest,' I squeaked faintly, and squeezed the ball again. 'I think I'm going to die,' said I, and I squeaked it every time I breathed." And Mr. Bowdoin gave audible demonstration of the squeak of his rubber toy. "Well, she was very remorseful, and she got up to send for the doctor; and faith, I had to get up and go downstairs after her and speak in my natural voice before she'd believe I wasn't in the last gasp of a croup. But she won't speak herself this morning," added the old gentleman rather ruefully. "What's the matter here?"

"Jamie has been down, and he says his son-in-law has decided to leave the bank."

"Dear me! dear me!" The old gentleman's face grew grave again. "Nothing wrong in his accounts, I hope?"

"He says that he has decided to go to New York to live."

"Go to New York! What'll become of the new house?"

"He has friends there. They are to sell the house."

" What 'll become of Jamie? "

" Jamie 's going back to Salem Street."

The old gentleman gave a low whistle. " I must see him," and he took his hat again and started up the street.

But from Jamie he learned nothing. The old man gave no reason, save that his son-in-law " was going to New York, where he had friends." It cost much to the old clerk to withhold from Mr. Bowdoin anything that concerned his own affairs, particularly when the old gentleman urged that he be permitted to use his influence to reinstate David at the bank. Jamie grew churlish, as was the poor fellow's manner when he could not be kind, and tried even to carry it off jauntily, as if St. Clair were bettering himself. Old Mr. Bowdoin's penetration went behind that, or he might have gone off in a huff. As it was, he half suspected the truth, and forbore to question Jamie further.

But it was harder still for the poor old clerk when he went home to Mercedes. For it was St. Clair who had sulked and refused to stay in Boston. He had hinted to his wife that it was due to Jamie's jealousy that he had lost

his place at the bank. Mercedes did not believe this; but she had thought that Jamie,
with his influence, might have kept him there.
More, she had herself, and secretly, gone to
the counting-room to see old Mr. Bowdoin, as
she had done once before when a child, and
asked that St. Clair might be taken back.
"Do you know why he lost the place?"

She did not. Perhaps he had been irregu-
lar in his attendance; she knew, too, that he
had been going to some horse-races.

"Jamie has not asked me to have him taken
back," said Mr. Bowdoin.

And she had returned, angry as only a loving woman can be, to reproach poor Jamie.
But he would never tell her of her husband's
theft. St. Clair was sharp enough to see this.
Jamie had settled the Worcester Square house
on Mercedes when they were married; and now
St. Clair got her to urge Jamie to sell it and
let him invest the money in a business opening
he had found in New York with some friends;
stock-brokerage he said it was. This poor
Jamie refused to do, and Mercedes forgave
him not. But St. Clair insisted still on going.
Perhaps he boasted to his New York friends of

his banking experience ; it was true that he had got some sort of an opening, with two young men of sporting tastes whom he had met.

Preparations for departure were made. The furniture was being taken out, and stored or sold ; and each piece, as it was carried down the stairs, brought a pang to Jamie's heart. The house was offered for sale ; Jamie drew up the advertisement in tears. He did not venture to sit with them now of evenings ; it was Jamie, of the three, who had the guilty feeling.

The evening before their going came. St. Clair was out at a farewell dinner, " tendered him," as he proudly announced, by his friends. Jamie, as he passed her door, heard Mercedes crying. He could not bear it ; he went in.

" My darling, do not cry," the old man whispered. " Is it because you are going away? All I can do for you — all I have shall be yours ! "

" What has David done? I know he has done something "—

" Nothing — nothing is wrong, dear ; I assure you "—

" Then why are you so hard to him? Why will you not put the money in the business ? "

Jamie was holding her hand. "My little Mercy," said he, "my little lady. Forgive me — do you forgive me?"

Mercedes looked at him, coldly perhaps.

"For the love of God, do not look like that! In the world or out of it, there's none I care for but just you, dear." Then Mercedes began to cry again, and kissed him. "And as for the money, dear, he'll have it as soon as I find the business is a decent one."

VIII.

Of course they had the money, and in some months the people at the bank began to hear fine accounts of St. Clair's doings in New York. Not so much, perhaps, from Jamie as from one or two other clerks to whom St. Clair had taken the trouble to write a letter or two. As for Jamie, he went back to live in the little house on Salem Street.

All the same, he grew thin and older-looking. He did not pretend to take the same interest in his work. Many and grave were the talks the two Bowdoins, father and son, had about him. The first few weeks after the departure of the St. Clairs, they feared actually for his life. He seemed to waste away. Then, one week, he went on to New York himself, and after that grew better. This was when he carried on to St. Clair the money coming from the sale of the house. Up to that time he had had no letter from Mercedes, though he wrote her every week.

He took care to place the money in Mercedes' name as special capital. But the other two men seemed to be active, progressive fellows. They reposed confidence in St. Clair, and they had always known him. After all, the old man tried to think, the qualities required to keep moneys separate were not those that went best to make it, and stock-broking was suited to a gambler as a business. For Jamie shared intensely the respectable prejudices against stock-broking of the elders of that day.

After this, he occasionally got letters from his Mercedes. They came addressed to the bank (as if she never liked to recognize that he was back in Salem Street), and it grew to be quite a joke among the other clerks to watch for them; for they had noticed their effect on

Jamie, and they soon learned to identify the handwriting which made him beam so that half the wrinkles went, and the old healthy apple-color came back to his cheeks.

Sometimes when the letter came they would place it under his blotter, and if it was a Tuesday (and she generally wrote for Tuesday's arrival) old Jamie's face would lengthen as he turned his mail over, or fall if he saw his desk empty. Woe to the clerk who asked a favor in those moments! Then the clerk next him would slyly turn the blotting-paper over, and Jamie would grasp the letter and crowd it into his pocket, and his face would gleam again. He never knew they suspected it, but on such occasions the whole bank would combine to invent a pretext for getting Jamie out of the room, that he might read his letter undisturbed. Otherwise he let it go till lunch-time, and then, they felt sure, took no lunch; for he would never read her letters when any one was looking on. They all knew who she was. It was the joke of years at the Old Colony Bank. They called Mercedes "old Jamie's foreign mail."

She never wrote regularly, however; and if

she missed, poor McMurtagh would invent most elaborate schemes, extra presents (he always made her an allowance), for extorting letters from her. The sight of her handwriting at any time would make his heart beat. Harley Bowdoin had by this time been taken into the counting-room. He was studying law as a profession (there being little left of the business), and Jamie appeared to be strangely fond of him. Often, by the ancient custom, he would call Harleston " Mr. James," Mr. James Bowdoin having no sons. Mr. James himself spoke of this intimacy once to his father. " Don't you see it 's because the boy fell in love with his Mercedes ? " said the old gentleman. Certain it is, the two were inseparable. One fancies Harleston heard more of Mrs. St. Clair than either of Jamie's older friends.

For Jamie, in her absence, grew to love all whom she had ever known, all who had ever seen her ; how much more, then, this young fellow who had shown the grace to love her, too ! Jamie was fond of walking to the places she had known, and he even took to going to church himself, to King's Chapel, where she had been so often. When his vacation came, the next summer, he went on to New York, and stayed at a cheap hotel on Fourth Avenue, and would go to see her; not too often, or when other people were there, for he was still modest, and only dared hope she might not hate him. It was all his fault, and perhaps he had been hard with her husband. But she suffered him now, and Jamie returned looking ten years younger. St. Clair seemed prosperous, and Jamie even mentioned his son-in-law to the other clerks, which was like a boast for Jamie.

Perhaps at no time had the two Bowdoins thought of him so much. He lived now as if he were very poor, and they suspected him of sending all his salary to Mercedes. "It makes no difference raising it; 't would all go just the same," said Mr. Bowdoin. "Man alive, why did n't you let him take the money, that day down the wharf, and take the girl yourself? You used to be keen enough about girls before you got so bald," added the old gentleman, with a chuckle. He was rather proud of his own shock of soft white hair.

"That 's why you were in such a haste to

marry me, I suppose," growled Mr. James. "You had no trouble of that kind yourself."

"Trouble? It's only your mother protects me. I was going down town in a 'bus to-day, and there I saw your mother coming out of one of those Abolition meetings of her cousin, Wendell Phillips, — I told her he 'd be hanged some day, — and there opposite sat an old gentleman, older than I, sir, and he said to me, 'Married, sir? So am I, sir. Married again only last week. Been married fifty years, but this one's a great improvement on the first one, sir, I can assure you. *She brushes my hair!*' That's more than you can get a wife to do for you, James!"

The father and son chirruped in unison.

"Did you tell my mother of your resolve to try again, sir?"

"I did, I did, and that my next choice was no incendiary Abolitionist, either. I told her I 'd asked her already, to keep her disengaged, — old Miss Virginia Pyncheon, you know; and, egad! if your mother did n't cut her to-day in the street! But what do you think of old Jamie?"

"I don't know what to think. He certainly seems very ill."

" Ah, James," said the old man, " why did you laugh that day ? If only the fairy stories about changing old clerks to fairy princes came true! She could not have married any one to love her like old Jamie."

IX.

Jamie had had no letter for many weeks. The clerks talked about it. Day by day he would go through the pile of letters on his desk in regular order, but with trembling fingers ; day by day he would lay them all aside, with notes for their answers. Then he would go for a moment into the great dark vault of the bank, where the bonds and stocks were kept, and come out rubbing his spectacles. The clerks would have forged a letter for him had they deemed it possible. There was talk even of sending a round-robin to Mrs. St. Clair.

It was a shorter walk from Salem Street than it had been from his daughter's mansion, and poor Jamie had not so much time each day to calculate the chances of a letter being there. Alas! a glance of the eye sufficed. Her notes were always on squarish white note-paper sealed in the middle (they still used no envelopes in those days), and were easy to see behind the pile of business letters and telegrams. And the five minutes of hope between breakfast and the bank were all old Jamie had to carry him through the day, for her letters never arrived in the afternoon.

But this foggy day Jamie came down conscious of a certain tremor of anticipation. It has been said that he had no religion, but he had ventured to pray the night before, — to pray that he might get a letter. He was wondering if it were not wrong to invoke the Deity for such selfish things. For the Deity (if there were one, indeed) seemed very far off and awful to Jamie. That there was anything trivial or foolish in the prayer did not occur to Jamie; it probably would have occurred to Mercedes.

But he got to the office at the usual time. The clerks were not looking at him (had he known it, a bad sign), and he cast his eye hastily over the pile. Then his face grew fixed once more. No letter from her was there, and he began to go through them all in routine order, the telegrams first.

The next thing that happened, the nearest clerk heard a sound and looked up, his finger on the column of figures and "carrying" 31 in his head. Old Jamie spoke to him. " I — I — must go out for an hour or two," he said. " I have a train to meet." His face was radiant, and all the clerks were looking up by this time. No one spoke, and Jamie went away.

" Did you see, he was positively blushing," said the teller.

There was a momentary cessation of all business at the bank. When old Mr. Bowdoin came in, on his way down to the wharf, he was struck at once with the atmosphere of the place.

" What 's the matter ? " he asked. " You look like you 'd all had your salaries raised."

" Old Jamie 's got his foreign mail," said the cashier.

But Jamie went out into the street to think of it undisturbed. It was a telegram : —

" Am coming on to-morrow. Meet me at five, Worcester depot.   MERCEDES."

She did not say anything about St. Clair, and Jamie felt sure he was not coming.

The fog had cleared away by this time, and

he went mechanically down to the old counting-room on the wharf. Harleston Bowdoin
was there alone, and Jamie found himself fa-
cing the young man before he realized where
his legs had carried him.

" What is it, Jamie ? " said Harley.

" She 's coming on to make me a visit," said
Jamie simply. " Mercedes — Mrs. St. Clair,
I mean." Then he wandered out, passing Mr.
Bowdoin on the stairs. He did not tell him
the news, and the old gentleman nearly choked
in his desire to speak of it. As he entered the
office, " Has he told you ? " cried Harleston.

" Has he told *you ?* " echoed the old gentleman. Harley told. Then Mr. Bowdoin turned
and bolted up the street after Jamie.

" Old fellow, why don't you have a vacation,
— just a few days ? The bank can spare you,
and you need rest." His hand was on the old
clerk's shoulder.

" Master Harley wull ha' told ye ? But
I 'm na one to neglect me affairs," said Jamie.

" Nonsense, nonsense. When is she coming ? "

Jamie told him.

" Why don't you take the one-forty and

meet her at Worcester? She may have to go back to-morrow."

Jamie started. It was clear he had not thought of this. As they entered the bank, Mr. Bowdoin cried out to Stanchion, the cashier, "I want to borrow McMurtagh for the day, on business of my own."

"Certainly, sir," said Mr. Stanchion.

Jamie went.

．　　．　　．　　．　　．　　．　　．　　．

There is no happiness so great as happiness to come, for then it has not begun to go. If the streets of the celestial city are as bright to Jamie as those of Boston were that day, he should have hope of heaven. It was yet two hours before his train went, but he had no thought of food. He passed a florist's; then turned and went in, blushing, to buy a bunch of roses. He was not anxious for the time to come, such pleasure lay in waiting. When at last the train started, the distance to Worcester never seemed so short. He was to come back over it with her!

In the car he got some water for his roses, but dared not smell of them lest their fragrance should be diminished. After reaching

Worcester, he had half an hour to wait; then the New York train came trundling in. As the cars rolled by he strained his old eyes to each window; the day was hot, and at an opened one Jamie saw the face of his Mercedes.

X.

The next morning, old Mr. James Bowdoin got up even earlier than usual, with an undefined sense of pleasure. As was his wont, he walked across the street to sit half an hour before breakfast in the Common. The old crossing-sweeper was already there, to receive his penny; and the orange-woman, expectant, sold her apex orange to him for a silver thripenny bit as his before-breakfast while awaiting the more dignified cunctation of his auguster spouse.

The old gentleman's mind was running on McMurtagh; and a robuster grin than usual encouraged even others than his chartered pensioners to come up to him for largess. Mr. Bowdoin's eyes wandered from the orange-woman to the telescope-man, and thence to an old elm with one gaunt dead limb that stretched out over the dawn. It was very pleasant that summer morning, and he felt no hurry to go in to breakfast.

Love was the best thing in the world; then why did it make the misery of it? How irradiated old Jamie's face had been the day before! Yet Jamie would never have gone to meet her at Worcester, had he not given him the hint. Dear, dear, what could be done for St. Clair, as he called himself? Mr. Bowdoin half suspected there had been trouble at the bank. Mercedes such a pretty creature, too! Only, Abby really never would do for her what she might have done. Why were women so impatient of each other? Old Mr. Bowdoin felt vaguely that it was they who were responsible for the social platform; and he looked at his watch.

Heavens! five minutes past eight! Mr. Bowdoin got up hurriedly, and, nodding to the orange-woman, shuffled into his house. But it was too late; Mrs. Bowdoin sat rigid behind the coffee-urn. Harley looked up with a twinkle in his eye.

"James, I should think, at your time of life, you 'd stop rambling over the Common

before breakfast, — in carpet slippers, too, —
when you know I 've been up so late the night
before at a meeting in behalf of " —

A sudden twinkle flashed over the old gentleman's rosy face ; then he became solemn,
preternaturally solemn. Harley caught the
expression and listened intently. Mrs. Bowdoin, pouring out cream as if it were coals of
fire on his head, was not looking at him.

" There ! " gasped old Mr. Bowdoin, dropping heavily into a chair. " Always said it
would happen. I feel faint ! "

" James ? " said Mrs. Bowdoin.

" Always said it would happen — and
there 's your cousin, Wendell Phillips, out on
the Common, hanging stark on the limb of an
elm-tree."

" *James !* "

" Always said it would come to this. Perhaps you 'd go out in carpet slippers if you
saw your wife's cousin hanged before your
eyes " —

" JAMES ! " cried Mrs. Bowdoin. But the
old lady was equal to the occasion ; she rose
(— " and no one there to cut him down ! "
interpolated the old gentleman feebly) and
went to the door.

The two men got up and ran to the window. There was something of a crowd around the old elm-tree ; and, pressing their noses against the pane, they could see the old lady crossing the street.

"I think, sir," said Mr. Harley to his grandfather, "it's about time to get down town." And they took their straw hats and sallied forth. But as they walked down the shady side of the street, old Mr. Bowdoin's progress became subject to impediments of laughter, which were less successfully suppressed as they got farther away, and in which the young man finally joined. "Though it's really too bad," he added, by way of protest, now laughing harder than his grandfather.

"I'm going to get her that carriage to-day," said the elder deprecatingly. Then, as if to change the subject, "Did you see old Jamie after he left, yesterday?"

"I think I caught him in a florist's, buying flowers," answered Harley.

"Buying flowers!" The old gentleman burst into such a roar that the passers in the crowded street stopped there to look at him, and went down town the merrier for it. "At a florist's! But what were you doing?" he closed, with sudden gravity.

"All right, governor, quite all right. I was buying them for grandma's birthday. *That*'s all over. Though I'm sorry for her, just the same. How does the man live, now?"

"Jamie says he's doing well," answered the other hurriedly. "By the way, stop at the bank and tell them to give old Jamie a holiday to-day. He'd never take it of himself."

"Are n't you coming down?" Harley spoke as he turned in by Court Square, — a poor neighborhood then, and surrounded by the police lodging - houses and doubtful hotels.

"Not that way," said Mr. Bowdoin. "I hate to see the faces one meets about there, poor things. Hope the flowers will get up to your grandmother, Harley; she'll need 'em!" And the old man went off with a final chuckle. "Hanging on a tree! Well, 't would be a good thing for the country if he were." Of such mental inconsistencies were benevolent old gentlemen then capable.

But when Harley reached the bank, though

it was late, Jamie had not yet arrived. Harley thought he knew the reason of this; but when old Mr. Bowdoin came, at noon, the clerk was still away; and the old gentleman, who had been merry all day, looked suddenly grave and waited. At one Jamie came in, hurrying.

"I hoped you would have taken a holiday to-day," said Mr. Bowdoin.

"I have come down to close the books," replied Jamie, not sharply. Mr. Bowdoin looked at him.

"Mr. Stanchion could have done that. Stanchion!"

"The books are nearly done, sir," said that gentleman, hurrying to the window.

"I prefer to stay, sir, and close the books myself, if Mr. Stanchion will forgive me." He spoke calmly; he gave both men a sudden sense of sorrow. Mr. Bowdoin accompanied him behind the rail.

"Come, Jamie, you need the rest, and Mercedes" —

"She has gone back, sir — and I — have business in New York. I must ask for three days off, beginning to-morrow."

"You shall have it, Jamie, you shall have it. But why did you not go back with Mercedes?"

Jamie made no reply but to bury his face in the ledger, and the old gentleman went away. The bank closed at two o'clock; by that time Jamie had not half finished his figuring. The cashier went, and the teller, each with a "good-night," to which Jamie hardly responded. The messenger went, first asking, "Can I help you with the safe?" to which Jamie gave a gruff "I am not ready." The day-watchman went, and the night-watchman came, each with his greeting. Jamie nodded. "You are late to-day." "I had to be." Last of all, Harley Bowdoin came in (one suspects, at his grandfather's request), on his way home from the old counting-room on the wharves.

"Still working, Jamie?"

"I must work until I finish, Mr. Harley."

"It's late for me," said Harley, "but a ship came in."

"A ship!"

"Oh, only the Maine Lady. Well, goodnight, Jamie."

"Good-night, Mr. Harley." Jamie had

never used the "Mr." to Harley before, of all the Bowdoins; and now it seemed emphasized, even. The young man stopped.

"Tell me, Jamie, can I help you in anything?"

"No!" cried old Jamie; and Harley fled.

Left alone, Jamie laid down his pen. It seemed his figuring was done. But he continued to sit, motionless, upon his high stool. For Mercedes had told him, between Worcester and Boston, that her David would be in prison, perhaps for life, unless he could get him seventeen thousand dollars within forty-eight hours.

She had pleaded with him all the way to Boston, all the way in the carriage down to the little house. His roses had been forgotten in the car. In vain he told her that he had no money.

She could not see that St. Clair had done anything wrong; it was a persecution of his partners, she said; the stock of a customer had been pledged for his own debt. Jamie understood the offense well enough. And then, in the evening, he had known that she was soon to have a child. But with this money all would be forgiven; and David would go back to New Orleans, where his friends urged him to return, "in his old profession." Could not Jamie borrow it, even? said Mercedes.

It was not then, but at the dawn, after a sleepless night, that Jamie had come to his decision. After all, what was his life, or his future, yes, or his honor, worth to any one? His memory, when he died, what mattered it to any one but Mercedes herself? And she would not remember him long. Was it not a species of selfishness — like his presumption in loving her — to care so for his own good name? So he had told Mercedes that he "would arrange it." After her burst of tears and gratitude, she became anxious about David; she feared he might destroy himself. So Jamie had put her on the morning train, and promised to follow that night.

The clock struck six, and the watchman passed by on his rounds. "Still there?"

"I 'm nearly done," said Jamie.

The cash drawer lay beside him; at a glance he saw the bills were there, sufficient for his purpose. He took up four rolls, each one having the amount of its contents marked on the paper band. Then he laid them on the desk again. He opened the day-book to make the necessary false entry. Which account was least likely to be drawn upon? Jamie turned the leaves rapidly.

"James Bowdoin's Sons." Not that. "The Maine Lady." He took up the pen, started to make the entry; then dashed it to the floor, burying his face in his hands.

He *could* not do it. The old bookkeeper's whole life cried out against a sin like that. To falsify the books! Closing the ledger, he took up the cash drawer and started for the safe. The watchman came in again.

"Done?" said he.

"Done," said Jamie.

The watchman went out, and Jamie entered the roomy old safe. He put the ledgers and the cash drawer in their places; but the sudden darkness blinded his eyes. In it he saw the face of his Mercedes, still sad but comforted, as he had left her at the train that morning.

He wiped the tears away and tried to think. He looked around the old vault, where so much money, idle money, money of dead people, lay mouldering away; and not one dollar of it to save his little girl.

Then his eye fell on the old box on the upper shelf. A hanged pirate's money! He drew the box down; the key still was on his bunch; he opened the chest. There the gold pieces lay in their canvas bag; no one had thought of them for almost twenty years. Now, as a thought struck him, he took down some old ledgers, ledgers of the old firm of James Bowdoin's Sons, that had been placed there for safe-keeping. He opened one after another hurriedly; then, getting the right one, he came out into the light, and, finding the index, turned to the page containing this entry: —

Dr. Pirates.

June 24, 1829: To account of whom it may concern (eagles, pistoles & doubloons) $16,897.00

He dipped his pen in ink, and with a firm hand wrote opposite: —

Cr.

June 22, 1848. By money stolen by James McMurtagh, to be accounted for $16,897.00

Then the old clerk drew a line across the account, returned the ledger to its place in the safe, and locked the heavy iron doors. The canvas bag was in his hands; the chest he had put back, empty.

PART THREE: RECOVERY.

I.

THE customer of St. Clair's firm was paid off, the partnership was dissolved without scandal, and the St. Clairs went to live in New Orleans. Jamie occupied one room in the attic of the old house in Salem Street. He wrote no more letters to Mercedes: he did not feel that he was worthy now to write to her. And a year or two after her arrival in New Orleans her letters ceased. She had thanked Jamie sorrowfully when he had paid over the money in New York, and kissed him with her pale lips (though his face was still paler), and upon the memory of this he had lived. But he had fancied her lips wore a new line; their curves had gone; and her eyes had certainly new depth.

When Mercedes ceased to write, Jamie did not complain. He knew well what the trouble was, and that her husband wished her to write to him for more money. But he could do no

more for her.   And after this his hope was
tired, and Jamie hardly had the wish to write.
The only link between them now was his
prayer at night.   The dry old Scotchman had
come to prayer at last, for her if not for
himself.

And the office lost their interest in him.
Only the Bowdoins were true.   For the " foreign mail " no longer came ; and Jamie was
no longer seen writing private letters on his
ledger page.   His dress grew so shabby that
old Mr. Bowdoin had to speak to him about
it.   He had no long absences at lunch-time,
but took a sandwich on the street.   In fact,
Jamie had grown to be a miser.

Great things were happening in those days,
but Jamie took no heed of them.   Human
liberty was in the air ; love of man and love of
law were at odds, and clashed with each other
in the streets ; Jamie took no heed of them.
They jostled on the pavement, but Jamie
walked to his task in the morning, and back
at night, between them ; seeing mankind but as
trees, walking ; bowed down with the love of
one.   And he who had never before thought
of self could think now only of his own dis-

honor. As a punishment, he tried not to think of her, except only at night, when his prayers permitted it; but he thought of her always. His crime made him ashamed to write to her; his single-heartedness made him avoid all other men.

Only one man, in all those years, did Jamie seem willing to talk to, at the office, and that man was Harleston Bowdoin. Had he not loved her? Jamie never spoke of her; but Harleston had a happy impulse, and would talk to the old man about Mercedes. Away from business, Jamie would walk in all the places where her feet had trod. He would go to King's Chapel Sundays; and he looked up John Hughson again, and would sit with him, wondering. John had married a stout wife, and had sturdy children. Hughson petted the old man, and gave him pipes of tobacco; for McMurtagh was too poor to buy tobacco, those days. The children on Salem Street feared him, as a miser; which was hard, for Jamie was very fond of little children.

How does a man live whose heart rules his soul, and is broken; whose conscience rules his head, and is dishonored? For men so

heavy laden, heaven was, and has been lost.
But Jamie never thought his soul immortal
until his love for Mercedes came into it ; perhaps not consciously now.   Such thoughts
would have seemed to him childish.   How,
then, did Jamie live ?   For no man can live
quite without hope, as we believe, — hope of
some event, some end of suffering, at least of
some worthier act.

With Jamie it was the hope of restitution.
He wished to leave behind him, as the score of
his life, that he had been true to his employer
and had loved his little ward.   And if the time
could ever come when he could do more for
her, it would not be until his theft was made
good, and his hands were free, as his heart, to
serve her again.   For the one thing that Jamie
stood for was integrity ; that was all the little
story of his life.

His salary was eighteen hundred dollars ; at
the end of the first year after his theft he had
spent a hundred and fifty.   Then he asked for
two days' leave of absence, and went to New
York, where he exchanged sixteen hundred
and forty dollars for Spanish gold pieces.   A
less old-fashioned man would have invested

the money at six per cent, but Jamie could not forego the satisfaction of restoring the actual gold. Coming back, he opened the old chest, now empty, one day, after hours, and put the pieces in the box. The naked gold made a shining roll in its blackness, just reaching across the lower end ; and poor Jamie felt the first thrill of — not happiness, but something that was not sorrow nor shame. And then he pulled down the old ledger, and made the first entry on the Dr. side : " Restored by James McMurtagh, June 9, 1849, $1640." The other ten dollars had gone for his journey to New York.

And that night, as he went home, he looked about him. He bowed (in his queer way) to one or two acquaintances who passed him, unconscious that he had been cutting them for a year. Before supper he went in to see John Hughson, carrying his pipe, and, without waiting to be offered it, asked to borrow a pinch of tobacco against the morrow, when he should buy some. The good Hughson was delighted, pressed a slab of "plug" upon him, and begged him to stay and have something liquid with his pipe. But Jamie would not ; he was anxious to be alone.

His little bedroom gave upon the roof of the adjoining house in the rear; and here his neighbor kept a few red geraniums in boxes, and it was Jamie's privilege to smoke his pipe among them. So this evening, after a hasty meal, he hurried up there. Beyond the roofs of the higher houses was a radiant golden sky, and in it the point of a crescent moon, and even as Jamie was lighting his pipe one star came.

Old. Jamie breathed hard and sighed, and the sigh meant rest. He took a pleasure in the tobacco, in the look of the sky again.

And with this throb of returning life, in one great pulsation, his love rushed back to his heart, and he thought of Mercedes. . . . He sat up nearly all the night, and with the first light of dawn he wrote to her.

II.

But Jamie got no answer to his letter, and he wrote again. Again he got no answer; and he wrote a third time, this time by registered mail; so that he got back a card, with her name signed to the receipt.

Jamie's manner, unconsciously to himself, had changed since that first row of gold coins had gone into the black tin box; the tellers and the bookkeepers had observed it, and they began to watch his mail again. What was their glee to see among Jamie's papers, one morning, a letter in the familiar feminine hand! "Jamie's foreign mail has come!" the word went round. "I thought it must be on its way," said the second bookkeeper; "have n't you noticed his looks lately?" "The letter is postmarked New Orleans," said the messenger boy, turning it over. But it was felt this went beyond friendly sympathy.

"Mr. O'Neill," said Mr. Stanchion sternly, "if I see you again interfering with McMurtagh's mail, you may go. What business is that of ours?"

Poor O'Neill hung his head, abashed. But all eyes were on Jamie as he opened his desk. He put the letter in his pocket. The clerks looked at one another. The suspense became unendurable. When old Mr. Bowdoin came in, the cashier told him what had happened. "Jamie's foreign mail has come again. But he will never read it here, sir, and we can't send him out till lunch-time : the chief book-keeper " —

The old gentleman's eyes twinkled. " Mc-Murtagh ! " he cried (Mr. Bowdoin had always called Jamie so since he came into the bank), " will you kindly step down to my counting-room ? I will meet you there in a few minutes, and there are some accounts I want you to straighten out for me."

As Jamie hurried down to the Long Wharf, he pressed his coat tight against him. The letter lay in his pocket, and he felt it warm against his breast.

Neither Mr. James Bowdoin nor Harley was in the little room (it was just as Jamie remembered it when he first had entered it, no pretense of business was made there now), and he tore the letter open. Thus it ran : —

NEW ORLEANS, *August* 30, 1849.

MY DEAR, DEAR JAMIE, — If I have not written to you it was only because I did not want to bring more trouble on you. But things have gone from bad to worse with us. I feel that I should be almost too unhappy to live, only that David is with me now. [Jamie

sobbed a little at this.] I wanted never to ask
you for money again. But we are very, very
poor. I will not give it to him. But if you
could send me a little money, a hundred dollars
would last me a long time.

　　　Your loving　　　M. St. Clair.

Jamie laid his head upon the old desk, and
his tears fell on the letter. What could he
do ? His conscience told him, nothing. All
his earnings belonged to the employers he had
robbed.

After a minute he took a sheet of paper and
tried to write the answer, no. And Mr. Bowdoin came in, and caught him crying. The
old gentleman knocked over a coal-scuttle, and
turned to pick it up. By the time he had
done so Jamie had rubbed the tears from his
eyes, and stood there like a soldier at " Atten-
tion."

" Jamie," said Mr. Bowdoin, " I should like
to make a little present to your ward, to Mercedes. Could you send it for me? I hope
she is well ? " And before Jamie could answer
Mr. Bowdoin had written out a check for a
hundred dollars. " Give her my love when

you write. I must go to a directors meeting."
And he scurried away hurriedly.

Jamie sat down again and wrote his letter,
and told her that the money was from Mr.
Bowdoin. " But, dear heart," it ended, " even
if I cannot help you, always write." And,
going home that night, Jamie began to fancy
that some omniscient power had put it into the
old gentleman's heart just then to do this
thing.

III.

Old Mr. Bowdoin, one morning, some time
after this, stood at his window before breakfast, drumming on the pane. The gesture has
commonly been understood to indicate discon-
tent with one's surroundings. Mrs. Bowdoin
had not yet come down to breakfast. Outside,
her worthy spouse could see the very tree upon
which cousin Wendell Phillips had not been
hanged ; and his mouth relaxed as he saw his
grandson Harley coming across the Common,
and heard the portentous creaking that at-
tended Mrs. Bowdoin's progress down the
stairs, — the butler supporting her arm, and
her maid behind attending her with shawl and

smelling-salts. The old lady was in a rude state of health, but had not walked a step alone for several years. As she entered, Harley behind her, old Mr. Bowdoin gravely and ostentatiously pulled out a silver dollar and put it into the hand of the surprised young man.

"Pass it to the account," said he.

Harley took the coin, and, detecting a wink, checked his expression of surprise.

"It all goes into the fund, my dear, to be given to your favorite charity the first time you are down in time for breakfast. It amounts to several thousand dollars already."

Mrs. Bowdoin snorted, but, with a too visible effort, only asked Harley whether he would take coffee or tea.

"With accumulations, my dear, — with accumulations. But you should not address me from your carriage in that yellow shawl, when I am talking to a stranger on the Common. At least, I thought it was Tom Pinckney, of the Providence Bank, but it turned out to be a stranger. He took me for a bunco-steerer."

"James!"

"He did indeed, and you for my confederate," chuckled the old gentleman. "'Mr. Pinckney, of Providence, I believe?' said I. 'No, you don't,' said he; and he put his finger on his nose, like that."

"James!" said Mrs. Bowdoin.

"*I* did n't mind — don't know when I 've been so flattered — must look like a pretty sharp old boy, after all, though I have been married to you for fifty years."

"James, it 's hardly forty."

"Well, I thought it was fifty. The last time I did meet Tom Pinckney, he asked if I 'd married again. I said you 'd give me no chance. 'Better take it when you can,' said he. 'That will I, Tom,' says I. 'I 've got one in my mind.'"

"Really, grandpa," remonstrated young Harley.

"Don't you talk, young man. Did n't I hear of you at another Abolition meeting yesterday? And women spoke, too, — short-haired women and long-haired men. Why can't you leave them both where a wise Providence placed them? Destroy the only free republic the world has ever known for a parcel of well-fed niggers that 'll relapse into Voodoo barbarism the moment they 're freed!"

"James, the country knows that the best sentiment of Boston is with us."

"The country does n't know Boston, then. And as for that crack-brained demagogue cousin of yours, he calls the Constitution a compact with hell! I hope I 'll live to see him hanged some day."

"Wendell Phillips is a martyr indeed."

"Martyr! Humbug! He could n't get any clients, so he took up a cause. Why, they say at the club that he " —

"They said at the meeting last night, sir," interrupted Harley, "that they 'd march up to the club and make you fellows fly the American flag."

"It 's Phillips wants to pull it down," said the old gentleman.

Mrs. Bowdoin rattled the tea things.

"Don't mind your grandma, Harley, if she is out of temper. She 's got a headache this morning. She went to bed with the hot-water bottle under her pillow and the brandy at her feet, and feels a little mixed."

"James! I never took a brandy bottle upstairs with me in my life. And Harleston knows " —

"Do you suppose he knows as well as I do, who have lived with you for fifty years?"

"And I'll not stay with you to hear my cousin insulted!" Majestic, she rose.

"It's too much of one girl," chuckled Mr. Bowdoin. "No wonder men keep a separate establishment."

"*James!*" Mrs. Bowdoin swept from the room.

"Don't run upstairs alone; consider the butler's feelings!" called her unfeeling spouse after her.

"You're too bad, sir," said Harley.

"I'm trying to develop her sense of humor; it's the one thing I always said I'd have in a wife. Remember it, when you get married. Why the devil don't you?"

"I have too much sense of humor, sir," said Harley gravely. "What is that?" For a noise of much shouting was heard from the Common. Both men rushed to the windows, and saw, surrounded by a maddened crowd, a small company of federal soldiers marching north.

"What are they saying?" cried Mr. Bowdoin.

Every minute the crowd increased: men and women, well dressed, sober-looking, crying, "Shame! shame!" and topping by a head the little squad of undersized soldiers (for the regular army was then recruited almost entirely from foreigners) who marched hurriedly forward, with eyes cast straight before and downward, and dressed in that shabby blue that ten years later was to pour southward in serried column, all American then, to free those slaves whom now they hunted down.

"To the Court House! To the Court House!" cried the mob.

"It's that fellow Simms," said Mr. Bowdoin, but was interrupted by sounds as of a portly person running downstairs; and they saw the front door fly open and Mrs. Bowdoin run across the street, her cap-strings streaming in the air.

"By Jove, if Abolitionism can make your grandma run, I'll forgive it a lot!" cried Mr. Bowdoin.

"Do you know the facts, sir?" suggested Harley.

"No, nor don't want to," said Mr. Bowdoin. "I know that we are jeopardizing the grandest experiment in free government the world has ever seen for a few African darkies that we did n't bring here, and have already made Christians of, and a d—d sight more comfortable than they ever were at home. But come, let 's go over, or I believe your grandma will be attacking the United States army all by herself ! "

But the rescue was made unnecessary by the return of that lady, panting.

" Now, sir," gasped Mrs. Bowdoin, " I hope you 're satisfied, that foreign Hessians control the laws of Massachusetts ! "

" I am always glad to see the flag of my country sustained," said Mr. Bowdoin dryly; " though we don't fly it from our club."

" I think you misunderstand, sir," ventured Harley. " This Simms is arrested by the Boston sheriff for stabbing a man ; and the Southerners have got the federal commissioner to refuse to give him up to justice."

" If he stabbed a man, it 's cheaper to let them sell him as a slave than keep him five years in our state prison."

" The poor man seems to prefer it though," said Harley gently. " Have you seen him ? "

"No; what should I see the fellow for?" cried Mr. Bowdoin irritably.

"I understand the State Court House is held like a fort by federal soldiers, and thugs who call themselves deputy marshals."

Mr. Bowdoin growled something that sounded like, "What if it is?"

The two started to walk down town. Tremont Street was crowded with running men, and School Street packed close; and as they came in sight of the Court House they saw that it was surrounded by a line of blue soldiers.

"Let's go to the Court House," said Harley.

The old gentleman's curiosity made feeble resistance.

"I had a case to see about this morning. Why, there's Judge Wells, the very man I want to see."

The judge had a body-guard of policemen, and our two friends joined him as they were slowly forcing a passage through the crowd. When they came before the old gray stone Court House, they saw two cannon posted at the corners, and all the windows full of armed troops; and around the base of the building, barring every door, a heavy iron cable, and behind this a line of soldiers.

"What the devil is the cable for?" said Mr. Bowdoin.

The crowd, which had opened to let the well-known judge go by, were now crying, "Let the judge in! Let the judge in!" and then, "Give him up! Give Simms up! Give him to the sheriff!" and then, "Kidnapped! Kidnapped!" Just ahead of them our party saw another judge stopped rudely before the door by a soldier dropping a bayonet across his breast.

"Can't get in here, — can't get in here."

"I tell you I'm a judge of the Supreme Court of this Commonwealth," they heard him say.

"Go around, then, and get under the chain. But the court can't sit to-day." Mr. Bowdoin bubbled with indignation as he saw the old man take off his high hat, and, stooping low, bow his white hairs to get beneath the chain.

"If I do, I'm damned," said Mr. Bowdoin quietly.

"And if I do, I'm — Drop it down, sir, and

let me pass: Judge Wells, of the Supreme Court of Massachusetts."

"And I 'm James Bowdoin, of James Bowdoin's Sons, and a good Democrat, and defendant in a confounded lawsuit before his honor."

" Courts can't sit to-day. Keep back."

" They can't? " cried Mr. Bowdoin. "Since when do the courts of Massachusetts ask permission of a pack of slave-hunters whether they shall sit or not? "

Harley was chuckling with suppressed delight. " If only grandma were here! " thought he.

"Let them in! Let Judge Wells in! " shouted the crowd.

The soldier called his corporal, and a hasty consultation followed; as a result of which the chain dropped at one end, and the three men walked over it in triumph.

"Three cheers for Judge Wells! Three cheers for Mr. Bowdoin! " cried the crowd, recognizing him.

When they got into the dark, cool corridor of the old stone fort, " That I should ever come to be cheered by a mob of Abolitionists!" gasped Mr. Bowdoin, mopping his face. "Upon my word, I think I lost my temper."

"Oh no, sir," said Harley Bowdoin gravely. "But where is the court-room?"

"Follow the line of soldiers," replied the judge, and hurried to his lobby.

Up the stone stairs went our friends, three flights in all; soldiers upon every landing, and, leaning over the banisters and carelessly spitting tobacco juice on the crowd below, a row of "deputy" United States marshals, with no uniform, but with drawn swords.

Mr. Bowdoin started. "Harley," said he, stopping by one of them, "I know that fellow. His name's Huxford, and he keeps a gambling-house; I had him turned out of one of my houses."

"Very likely," said Harley.

"Move on there, move on," said the man surlily, pretending not to recognize Mr. Bowdoin.

"What are you doing here, sir?" said that gentleman. "Don't you know I swore out a warrant against you?"

"Who the h—l are you?"

"James Bowdoin, confound you!" answered

that peppery person, and swung his fist right and left with such vigor that Huxford went down on one side, and another deputy on the other. Then Harley hurried the old gentleman through the breach into the upper courtroom, where they were under the protection of the county sheriff in his swallow-tailed blue coat, cocked hat, gold lace, and sword, and a friendly judge.

"Hang it, sir, they 'll be arresting you, next," said Harley.

"By Heaven, I should like to see them do it!" cried our old friend in a loud whisper, if the term can be used. "Sheriff Clark, do you know those fellows are all miserable loafers?"

"They are federal officers, sir; I can do nothing," whispered back that gorgeous official.

"Humph!" returned Mr. Bowdoin. "How about state rights? Do we live in the sovereign State of Massachusetts, or do we not, I should like to know?"

"How about the Union, sir?" whispered Harley slyly.

"Hang the Union! Hang the Union, if it

employ a parcel of thugs to do its work ! " said Mr. Bowdoin, so loud that there was a ripple of laughter in the court-room; and the judge looked up from the bench and smiled, for had not he dined with old Mr. Bowdoin in their college club once a month for forty years? But a low-browed fellow who was sitting behind the counsel at the table was heard to mutter " Treason." Beside him in the prisoner's dock sat the slave; not cowed nor abject, though in chains and handcuffs, but looking straight before him at the low-browed man who was his master, as a bird might look at a snake.

" Which of those two is the slave ? " asked Mr. Bowdoin in an audible voice.

Again the room laughed. The clerk rapped order. The low-browed man looked up angrily, and spoke to a deputy marshal whose face had been turned away from Mr. Bowdoin before. He rose and started toward them.

" By Heaven," cried Mr. Bowdoin, " it is David St. Clair ! "

IV.

But old Jamie knew naught of this, and the Bowdoins never told him. They consulted much what they should do; but they never told him. And Jamie went on, piling up his money. Three rolls were in the old chest now, and all of Spanish gold. Doubloons and pistoles were growing rarer, and the price was getting higher. But the old clerk was not content with replacing the present value to the credit of " Pirates " on the books; the actual pieces must be returned; so that if any earringed, whiskered buccaneer turned up to demand his money from James Bowdoin's Sons, he might have it back in specie, in the very pieces themselves, that the honor of the firm might be maintained. Until then, he felt sure, there was little chance the box would ever be looked into. Practically, he was safe; it was only his conscience, not his fears, that troubled him.

Since he had sent her that hundred dollars, he had heard nothing from Mercedes. The Bowdoins did not tell him how her husband had sunk to be a slave-catcher; for they knew

how miserly old Jamie had become, and supposed that his salary all went to her. While
Jamie could take care of her, it mattered little
what the worthless husband did, save the pain
of Jamie's knowing it. And of course they
did not know that Jamie could no longer take
care of her, and why.

But one day, in the spring of 185-, a New
York correspondent of the bank came on to
Boston, and Mr. Bowdoin gave a dinner for
him at the house. The dinner was at three
o'clock; but old lady Bowdoin wore her best
gown of tea-colored satin, and James Bowdoin
and his wife were there. After dinner, the
three gentlemen sat discussing old madeira,
and old and new methods of banking, and the
difference between Boston and New York,
which was already beginning to assume a
metropolitan preëminence.

"By the way, speaking of old-fashioned
ways," said the New Yorker suddenly, "that 's
a queer old clerk of yours, — Mr. McMurtagh,
I mean."

"Looks as if he might have stepped out of
one of Dickens's novels, does he not?" said
Mr. Bowdoin, always delighted to have Jamie's
peculiarities appreciatively mentioned.

" But how did you come to know him?"
asked Mr. James.

" Why, I see him once a year or so. Don't
you send him occasionally to New York?"

" He used to go, some years ago," said Mr.
Bowdoin.

" He buys his Spanish gold of us," added
the New Yorker. " Queer fancy you have of
buying up doubloons. Gold is gold, though,
in these times."

" Spanish doubloons?" said Mr. James.

" We have a use for them at the bank,"
remarked the old gentleman sharply. " Shall
we join the ladies?"

" You have to pay a pretty premium for
them," added the money-dealer, as he stopped
to wipe his lips. " Wonderful madeira, this."

Old Mr. Bowdoin took no squeaking toy to
bed with him that night; but at breakfast his
worthy spouse vowed he must take another
room if he would be so wakeful. For once
the old gentleman had no repartee, but hurried
down to the bank. Early as he was, he found
his son James there before him. And with
all his soul he seized upon the chance to lose
his temper.

" Well, sir, and what are you spying about
for ?   You 're not a director in the bank ! "

Mr. James looked up, astonished.

" Got a headache, I suppose, from drinking
with that New York tyke they sent us yesterday ! "

" Well, sir, when it comes to old madeira " —

" I earned it, I bought it, and I can drink
it, too.   And as for your Wall Street whipper-
snappers that have n't pedigree enough to get
a taste for wine, and drink champagne, and
don't know an honest man when they see one
— it 's so seldom " —

" Seriously, what do you suppose he wanted
with the gold ? "

" I don't know, sir, and I don't care.   But
since you 're spying round, come in ! " and
Mr. Bowdoin led his son into the vault.
" There, sir, there 's the confounded box,"
tapping with his cane the old chest that lay on
the top shelf.

" I see, sir," said Mr. James, taking his cue.

" And as for its contents, the firm of James
Bowdoin's Sons are responsible.   Perhaps
you 'd like to poke your nose in there ? "

"Oh no, sir," said Mr. James. And that chest was never opened by James Bowdoin or James Bowdoin's Sons.

"When the pirate wants it, he can have it, — in hell or elsewhere," ended Mr. Bowdoin profanely.

But coming out, and after Mr. James had gone away, the old gentleman went to Jamie McMurtagh's desk. Poor Jamie had seen them enter the vault, and his heart stood still. But all Mr. Bowdoin said was to ask him if his salary was sufficient. For once in his life the poor old man had failed to meet his benefactor's eye.

"It is quite enough, sir. I — I deserve no more."

But Mr. Bowdoin was not satisfied. "Jamie," he said, "if you should ever need more money, — a good deal of money, I mean, — you will come to me, won't you? You could secure it by a policy on your life, you know."

Jamie's voice broke. "I have no need of money, sir."

"And Mercedes? How is she?"

"It is some time since I heard, sir; the last

was, she had gone with her husband to Havana."

"Havana!" shouted Mr. Bowdoin; and before Jamie could explain he had crushed his beaver on his head and rushed from the bank.

Jamie's head sank over the desk, and the tears came. If only this cup could pass from him! If Heaven would pardon this one deceit in all his darkened, upright life, and let him restore the one trust he had broken, before he died! And then he dried his eyes, and took to figuring, — figuring over again, as he had so often done before, the time needed, at the present rate, to make good his theft. Ten years more — a little less — would do it.

But old Mr. Bowdoin ran to the counting-room, where he found his son and Harley in that gloomy silence that ends an unsatisfactory communication.

"Say what you will, you'll never make me believe old Jamie is a thief," said Harley.

"Thief! you low-toned rascal!" cried Mr. Bowdoin. "Thief yourself! He's just told me Mercedes is in Havana. Of course he wants Spanish gold!"

"Of course he does!" cried Harley.

" Of course he does ! " cried James.

Their faces brightened, and each one in-
wardly congratulated himself that the others
had not thought how much easier it would
have been for Jamie to send her bills of exchange.

V.

Meantime, Jamie, all unconscious of his
patrons' anxiety, went on, from spring to fall
and fall to spring, working without hope of
her, to make his honor good to men. If there
was one day in the year that could be said to
bring him near enjoyment, it was that day
when, his yearly salary saved, he went to New
York to buy doubloons. One might almost
say he enjoyed this. He enjoyed the night
voyage upon the Sound ; the waking in the
noisy city by busy ships that had come, perhaps, from New Orleans or Havana; the
crowded streets, with crowds of which she had
once been one, crowds so great that it seemed
they must include her still. The broker of
whom he bought his gold would always ask to
see him, and offer him a glass of wine, which,
taken by Jamie with a trembling hand, would

bring an unwonted glow to his wrinkled cheeks as he hastened away grasping tight his canvas bag of coin. The miser!

Can you make a story of such a life? It had its interest for the recording angel. But it was two years more to the next event we men must notice.

May the twenty-seventh, eighteen fifty-four. Old Jamie (old he had been called for thirty years, and now was old indeed) had finished his work rather early and locked up the books. All day there had been noise and tramping of soldiers and murmurs of the people out on the street before the door, but Jamie had not noticed it. Old Mr. Bowdoin had rushed in and out, red in the face as a cherry, sputtering irascibility, but Jamie had not known it. And now he had come from counting his coin, a pleasure to him, so nearly the old chest lay as full as it had been that day a quarter century before. He had been gloating over it with a candle in the dark vault; but a few rows more, and his work was done, and he might go — to die, or find Mercedes.

As he came out into the street, blinking in

the sudden sunlight, he found it crowded close
with quiet people. So thick they stood, he
could not press his way along the sidewalk.
It was not a mob, for there was no shouting
or disorder; yet, intermittently, there rose a
great murmur, such as the waves make or the
leaves, the muttering of a multitude. Jamie
turned his face homeward, and edged along by
the wall, where there was most room. And
now the mutter rose and swelled, and above
it he heard the noise of fife and drum and the
tread of soldiers.

He came to the first cross-street, and found
it cleared and patrolled by cavalry militia.
The man on a horse in front called him by
name, and waved his sword at him to pass.
Jamie looked up, and saw it was John Hughson. He would not have known him in his
scarlet coat.

"What is it, John?" said Jamie.

"What is it? The whole militia of the
State is out, by G—! to see them catch and
take one nigger South. Look there!"

And Jamie looked from the open side street
up the main street. There, beneath the lion
and the unicorn of the old State House,

through that historic street, cleared now as for a triumph, marched a company of federal troops. Behind them, in a hollow square, followed a body of rough-appearing men, each with a short Roman sword and a revolver; and in the open centre, alone and handcuffed, one trembling negro. The fife had stopped, and they marched now in a hushed silence to the tap of a solitary drum; and behind came the naval marines with cannon.

The street was hung across with flags, union down or draped in black, but the crowd was still. And all along the street, as far down as the wharf, where the free sea shone blue in the May sunshine, stood, on either side, a close rank of Massachusetts militia, with bayonets fixed, four thousand strong, restraining, behind, the fifty thousand men who muttered angrily, but stood still. Thus much it took to hold the old Bay State to the Union in 1854, and carry one slave from it to bondage. Down the old street it was South Carolina that walked that day beneath the national flag, and Massachusetts that did homage, biding her time till her sister State should turn her arms upon the emblem. "Shame! shame!" the people were crying. But they kept the peace of the republic.

Old Jamie understood nothing of this. He only saw and wondered; saw the soldiery, saw old Mr. Bowdoin leaning from a window as a young man on the sidewalk tried to drag down a flag that hung from it, with a black coffin stitched to the blue field.[1]

"Young man," cried the old gentleman, "leave that flag alone; it's my property!"

"I am an American," cried the youth, "and I'll not suffer the flag of my country to be so disgraced!"

"I too am an American, and damme, sir, 't is the flag in the street there that's disgraced!"

The fellow slunk away, but Jamie had ceased to listen, for the negro was now in front of him, and there, among the rough band of slave-catchers, his desperate appearance hid by no uniform, a rough felt hat upon his dissolute face, a bowie-knife slung by his waist, there, doing this work in the world, old Jamie saw and recognized the husband of his little girl, — St. Clair.

---

[1] A fact, but the man who thus assaulted the flag lived to command a company in the Union army.

VI.

McMurtagh ran out into the street toward him, but was stopped by an officer. He still pressed his way, and when the end of the procession went by they suffered him to go, and he fell in behind the trailing cannon. There he found some others, following out of sympathy for the slave. Some of them he knew, and they took Jamie for an Abolitionist, but Jamie hardly knew what it was all about.

"When Simms was taken," said one, a doctor, "I vowed that he should be the last slave sent back from Massachusetts."

"Did you hear," said another, a young lawyer, "how they have treated him? His master had him whipped, when he got home, for defending his case before our courts."

Jamie tried to find his way through the artillery company, but failed. It was only when they got down to the Long Wharf that the artillery divided, sending two guns to either side of the street, and Jamie and the others hurried to the end. Here was a United States revenue cutter, armed with marines, to take this poor bondsman back to his master.

No crowned head ever left a country with more pomp of escort and retinue of flag and cannon. But Jamie's business was with the slave-catcher, not the slave. He found St. Clair standing by the gangway, and called him by name. The fellow started like a criminal; then recognizing the poor clerk, " Oh, it 's you, is it ? "

"How is Mercedes?" stammered Jamie.

" How the h—l should I know? And what is that to you?"

" But you will tell me where she is?" pleaded the poor old man. "She will not answer my letters. Does she get them? I know she does not get them," he added, as the thought struck him suddenly.

"She gets any that have got money in," retorted St. Clair grimly. " However, I married her, and I suppose I 've got to support her. Get out of the way, there!"

The men were already casting off the ropes. Poor Jamie felt in his pocket, but of course he had no money; he never carried money now.

The cordon of soldiers drew across the wharf and presented arms as their commanding officer came ashore, and the stars and stripes rose at the stern of the vessel, and she forged out toward the blue rim of the sea that is visible, even from the wharves, in Boston harbor.

But not a gun was fired. Silently the armed ship left, with its freight of one negro, its company of marines and squad of marshals. Among them St. Clair stood on the lower deck and looked at Jamie. The poor clerk hung his head as if he were the guilty one. And in the silence was heard the voice of a minister in prayer. The little group of citizens gathered around him with bared heads. He prayed for the poor slave and for the recreant republic, for peace, and that no slave-hunter should again tread quietly the soil of Massachusetts. But Jamie heard him not. He was thinking over again the old trouble: how he could not take his salary — that was needed for restitution; how he could not ask the Bowdoins, or they would wonder where his salary had gone.

As he turned his steps backward to the city, he wondered if St. Clair was still living with her. But yes, he must be, or she would surely have come back to him. A hand was laid upon

his shoulder; he looked up; it was the minister who had been upon the wharf.

"Be not cast down, old man. 'In his service is perfect freedom,'" quoted the minister.
He fancied he was one of the Abolitionist
group that had followed Anthony Burns to the
last. But Jamie only looked up blankly. He
was thinking that in four years more he might
go to bring back Mercedes.

VII.

Year followed year. This was the twelfth
year since Jamie had begun to make up his
theft from his own salary; but it had been
slower work than he had hoped, for he now
had to pay almost a collector's price to get the
Spanish gold. He had hurried home one night
eagerly, to count his money; for he made his
annual purchase and payment in June. Sixteen hundred dollars in bills he had (it was
curious that he kept it now in money, and had
no longer a deposit in the bank), and he congratulated himself that he had not had the
money at the wharf that day: he might have
given it to St. Clair, to learn Mercedes' where-

abouts; and it would not have reached her, and St. Clair would have lied to him; while the taking of a dollar more than was rightfully the bank's — for so Jamie regarded his salary — would really make him a defaulter.

For the old chest was getting so full now that the clerk could almost hold his head up among men. The next year, but three rows of gold coin remained to fill. The smaller coins had all been purchased long ago. And Jamie (who had only thought to do this, and die, at the first) now began, timidly, to let his imagination go beyond the restitution; to think of Mercedes, of seeing her, of making her happy yet. For she was still a young girl, to him.

The thirteenth year came. Jamie had begun to take notice of the world. He took regularly a New Orleans newspaper. The balance against him in the account was now so small! He looked wistfully at the page. However small the deficit, his labors were not complete till he could tear the whole page out. And he could not do that yet : the transaction must be shown upon the books ; he might die.

Die! Suddenly his heart beat at the

thought. Die! He had never thought of this, to fear it; but now if he should die before the gold was all returned, and all his sacrifice go for naught, even his sacrifice of Mercedes —

The other clerks had lost their interest in poor Jamie by this time; some of them were new, and to these he was merely an old miser, and they made fun of him, he grew so careful about his health. Life had not brought much to poor Jamie to make him so fond of it; but both the Bowdoins noticed it, and remarked to one another, it was curious, after all, how men clung to life as they grew older.

In 1859 a rumor had reached them all that St. Clair had gone on some filibustering expedition to Cuba. Old Mr. Bowdoin mentioned it to McMurtagh; but he said nothing of sending for the wife. In 1861 the war broke out, and the poor clerk saw the one sober crown of his life put off still a year. He was yet more than a thousand dollars short. He was coming back ou a Sound steamer, thinking of this, wondering how he could bear this last delay, — his scanty bag of high-priced gold crowded into a pocket, — reading his New Orleans paper carelessly (save only the births and deaths), when his eye caught a name. Jamie knew there was a war; and the article was all about some fighting of blockade-runners with a federal cruiser near Mobile. But his quick eye traveled to the centre of it, where he read, "Before the vessel was taken, a round shot killed several of the crew, . . . among them . . . and David St. Clair, well known in this city."

VIII.

Jamie could not go to bed that night, but sat on deck watching the stars. The next day he went through his avocations in the bank like one in a dream. And in the night ensuing that dream became a vision; and he saw Mercedes alone in a distant city, without money or friends, her soft eyes looking wistfully at him in wonder that he did not come.

The next morning Jamie went to old Mr. Bowdoin's office, at an hour when he knew he should find him alone. For the old gentleman called early at the little counting-room, as in the days when he might hope to find some ship of his own, fresh from the Orient, warping into the dock. Jamie's lips were dry, and his

voice came huskily. He gave up the effort to
speak of St. Clair's death, but asked briefly
that Mr. Bowdoin would get him three months'
leave.

"Three months!" cried the old man.
"Why, Jamie, you've not taken a vacation
for fifteen years!"

"That's why I make bold to ask it, sir,"
said Jamie humbly.

"Take six months, man, six months, — not
a week less! And your salary shall be paid
in advance" — Mr. Bowdoin noted a sudden
kindling in Jamie's eye that gave him his cue.
"Two quarters! you have well deserved it.
And now that the bank is to change its charter,
there'll be a lot of fuss and worry; it'll be a
good time to go away."

"Change its charter?"

"Ay, Jamie; we've got to give up being a
state bank, and go in under the new national
law to issue shinplasters to pay for beating
the rebels! But come with me to the bank,
— the board are meeting now for discounts,"
and the old gentleman grabbed his hat, and
dragged Jamie out of the counting-room.

I doubt if ever the old clerk was rushed so

rapidly up the street. And coming into the bank, Mr. Bowdoin shoved him into an anteroom. "Wait you there!" said he, and plunged into the board-room.

There had been a light spring snow that night, and Jamie had not had time to wipe his boots. He cleaned them now, and then went back and sat upon a sofa near the sacred precincts of the directors' room. Suddenly he felt a closing of the heart; he wondered if he were going to be taken into custody — after so many years — and now, just now, when he must go to rescue Mercedes. Then he remembered that he had been brought there by Mr. Bowdoin, and Jamie knew better than to think this.

In a minute more the door opened, and that gentleman came out. Behind him peered the faces of the directors; in his hand was a crisp new bank-note.

"McMurtagh," said Mr. Bowdoin, "the directors have voted to give you a six months' vacation; and as some further slight recognition of your twenty years of service, this," and he thrust a thousand-dollar note into his hand.

Jamie's labors were light that day. To

begin with, every clerk and teller and errand-
boy had to shake him by the hand and hear
all about it. And it was not for the money's
sake. Old Mr. Bowdoin had been shrewd
enough to guess what only thing could make
the clerk want so much liberty; and the news
had leaked down to the others, — " that Jamie
was going for his foreign mail."

" I hear you are going away," said one.
" To Europe ? " said another. " Blockade-
running ! " suggested a third. " For cotton."

" I — I am going to the tropics," stammered
Jamie. He had but a clouded notion how far
south New Orleans might be.

" I told you so," laughed the teller.

" Bring us all a bale or two."

Jamie laughed; to the amazement of the
bank, Jamie laughed.

When the cashier went to lunch, Jamie stole
a chance to get into the vault alone. And
there, out of every pocket, with trembling
fingers, he pulled a little roll of Spanish gold.
Then the delight of sorting and arranging
them in the old chest! He had one side for
pistoles, and this now was full; and even the
doubloon side showed less than the empty

space of one roll, across the little chest, needed to fill the count, after he had put the new coins in. The old clerk sat in a sort of ecstasy; reminding himself still that what he gazed at was not the greatest joy he had that day; when all these sordid things were over, he was to start, on the morrow, for Mercedes.

He heard the voice of the cashier returning, and went out.

"Well, McMurtagh," said he, "you're lucky to escape this miserable reorganization. July 1st we start as a national bank, you know."

"Yes," said Jamie absently.

"Every stick and stone in this old place has got to be counted over again, the first of the month, by the examiners of Uncle Sam, and every book verified. By the way," the cashier ended carelessly, as witless messengers of fate alone can say such things, "you'd better leave me the key of that old chest we carry in special account for the Bowdoins. They'll want to look at everything, you know. The examination may come next year, or it may come any time."

IX.

A few minutes more of Jamie's life were added to the forty years he had spent over his desk. He even went through a few columns of figures. Then he closed the desk, leaving his papers in it as usual, and went out into the street.

So it was all gone for naught, — all his labors, all his self-denial, all his denial of help to Mercedes. If he left to seek her, his theft would be discovered in his absence. He would be thought to have run away, to have absconded, knowing his detection was at hand. If he stayed, he could not make it good in time.

What did it matter? She was first. Jamie took his way up the familiar street, through the muddy snow; it had been a day of foul weather, and now through the murky low-lying clouds a lurid saffron glow foretold a clearing in the west. It was spring, after all; and the light reminded Jamie of the South. She was there, and alone.

He had tried to save his own good name, and it was all in vain. He might at least do what he could for her.

He did not go home, but wandered on, walking. Unconsciously his steps followed the southwest, toward the light (we always walk to the west in the afternoon), and he found himself by the long beach of the Back Bay, the railroad behind him. The tide was high, and the west wind blew the waves in froth at his feet. The clearing morrow sent its courier of cold wind; and the old clerk shivered, but did not know he shivered of cold.

He sat upon an old spar to think. The train bound southward rattled behind him; he was sitting on the very bank of the track, so close that the engineer blew his whistle; but Jamie did not hear. So this was the end. He might as well have saved her long before. He might have stolen more. To-morrow he would surely go.

The night came on. Then Jamie thought of getting his ticket. He remembered vaguely that the railroad behind him ran southward; and he rose, and walked along the track to the depot. There he asked if they sold tickets to New Orleans.

The clerk laughed. New Orleans was within the rebel lines. Besides, they sold no tickets beyond New York or Washington. The clerk did not seem sure the way to New Orleans was through Washington. A ticket to the latter city was twenty dollars.

Jamie pulled out his wallet. He had only a few dollars in it; but loose in his pocket he found that thousand-dollar bill. "I — I think I will put off buying the ticket until to-morrow," he said.

For a new notion flashed upon him. He had not thought of this money before. With what he could earn, — the bookkeeper had said the investigation might be put off a year, — this bill might be enough to cover the remaining deficit.

He hugged it in his hands. How could he have forgotten it? He turned out into the night again to walk home; he felt very faint and cold, and remembered he had had no supper. Well, old Mrs. Hughson would get him something. She had taken the little house on Salem Street, which had been Jamie's home for so many years. John and his growing family still lived in their house, near by.

But Mrs. Hughson was out. He stumbled up the high stairs in the dark, and lit a lamp with numbed fingers. He had not been often so late away; probably she had gone to search for him. He must go out after her. She was doubtless at John's.

But first McMurtagh went to his writing-desk and unlocked the drawer that he had not visited for years; and from its dust, beneath a pile of letters, he drew out his only picture of Mercedes. He had vowed never to look at it again until he could go to help her; and now —

And now he was not going to help her. He had left her alone all those years; and now he was still to leave her, widowed, in a hostile city, perhaps to starve. Old Jamie strained his eyes to the picture with hard tearless sorrow. It was a daguerreotype of the beautiful young girl that Mercedes had been in 1845.

Was there no way? The thousand dollars he would need if he went after her. Should he borrow of Mr. Bowdoin? But how could he do so, now that he had this present from him? Jamie sat down and pressed his fingers to his temples. Then he forgot himself a moment.

He was out in the street again in the cold.

He had the idea that he would go to John
Hughson's ; and sure enough, he found the old
lady there. She and John cried out as he
came in, and would know where he had been.
He could not tell. " Why, you are cold," said
the old lady, feeling his hand. And they
would have him eat something.

In the street again, returning : it was pleas-
anter in the dark ; one could think. One
could think of her ; he dared not when people
were looking, lest they should know. He
would go to her.

Suppose he told old Mr. Bowdoin, frankly,
the debt was nearly made up : he would gladly
lend him. Nay, but it was a theft, not a debt.
How could he tell — now — when so nearly
saved ?

In the room, Mrs. Hughson was bustling
about getting a hot drink. So nearly ! Why,
even if David might have lived a year more !
And he had been a slave-catcher. Perhaps he
had left her money ? Perhaps she might get
on for a year — if he wrote ? Ah, here was
the hot drink. He would take it ; yes, if only
to get rid of Mrs. Hughson. She looked old
and queer, and smiled at him. But he did not

know Mercedes' address; he could not write.
Yes, he felt warmer now; he was well enough,
thank you. Ah, by Heaven, he would go!
He must sleep first. Would not Mrs. Hughson put out the light? He liked it better
so. Good-night. Just this rest, and then the
palm-trees, and such a sunny, idle sky, where
Mercedes was walking with him. The account had been nearly made up; the balance
might rest.

X.

No letter came back from Jamie, and Mr.
Bowdoin rather wondered at it. But openly
he pooh-poohed the idea. His wife had lost
twenty years of her age in presiding over San-
itary Commissions, and getting up classes
where little girls picked lint for Union soldiers; and Mr. Bowdoin himself was full of
the war news in the papers. For he was a
war Democrat (that fine old name!), and had
he had his way, every son and grandson would
have been in the Union army. Most of them
were, among them Harley, though the family
blood had made him choose the naval branch.
Commander Harleston Bowdoin was back on

a furlough won him by a gunshot wound : and it was he who asked about old Jamie most anxiously.

" You feel sure that he was going to Havana ? " said he over the family breakfast table.

Old lady Bowdoin had left them ; long since she had established her claim to the donation fund by arriving always first at breakfast, and had devoted it, triumphantly, to a fund for free negroes, — " contrabands," as they were just then called. But Mrs. Bowdoin never had taken much interest in Mercedes.

" Sure, they were last heard of there. He was on some filibustering expedition in Cuba. Perhaps he was hanged. But no, I don't think so. Poor Jamie used to send them so much money ! "

" He might have written before he sailed," said Harley, nursing his wounded arm.

" If he wrote, I guess he wrote to her," said Mr. Bowdoin dryly. " Why should he write to me ? "

" I don't like it," said Harley.

Mr. Bowdoin did not like it ; and not being willing to admit this to himself, it made him very cross. So he rose, and, crowding his hat over his eyes, strode out into the April morning, and down the street to the wharf, and down the wharf to the office, where he silenced his trio of pensioners for the time being by telling them all to go to the devil; *he* would not be bothered. And these, hardly surprised, and not at all offended, hobbled around to the southern side of the building, where they lent each other quarters against the morrow, when they knew the peppery old gentleman would relent.

Mr. Bowdoin stamped up the two flights of narrow stairs to the counting-room, where his first action was to take off a large piece of cannel coal just put on the fire by Mr. James Bowdoin, and damn his son and heir for his extravagance. As the coal put back in the hod was rapidly filling the room with its smoke, James the younger fled incontinently; and the elder contemplated the situation. It was true Jamie had not written; but he had not thought much about it. Harley entered.

"I was thinking, sir, of going down to Mr. McMurtagh's lodgings and asking if they had heard from him."

"Have n't you been there yet? I should think any fool would have gone there first!"

"That 's why I did n't, sir," said Harley respectfully.

Old Mr. Bowdoin chuckled grimly, and his grandson took his leave.

"Come back and tell me at the bank!" cried Mr. Bowdoin.

But hardly had Harley got down the stairs before the old gentleman had another visitor. And this time it was a sheriff with brass buttons; and he held a large document in his hands.

Now Mr. Bowdoin was not over-fond of officers of the law; he detested lawsuits, and he had a horror of legal documents. Therefore he groaned at the sight, and, throwing open a window, fingered his watch-chain nervously, as one who is about to flee.

"What do *you* want, sir?" said he.

"Is this the office of James Bowdoin's Sons?"

"What if it were, sir?"

The officer brandished his document. "Is there a clerk here, — one James McMurtagh?"

"No, sir." Mr. Bowdoin spoke decidedly.

"Has he a son-in-law, David St. Clair?"

The old gentleman breathed a sigh of relief. "He has, sir."

"Where is McMurtagh?"

"I don't know, sir."

"Where is St. Clair?"

"Have you a citation for him?"

The officer winked. "Can you tell me where to find him?"

Mr. Bowdoin saw his chance. "Yes, sir; I can, sir. The last I heard of him, he had gone to Cuba on a filibustering expedition with one General Walker, who has since been hanged; and if you find him, you 'll find him in Havana, Cuba, and can serve the citation on him there; though I 'm bound to tell you," ended the old gentleman in a louder voice, "my opinion is, he won't care a d—n for you or your citation either!" And Mr. Bowdoin bolted down the stairs.

XI.

So Mr. Bowdoin hurried up the street to the bank, half chuckling, half angry, still.

Then (having found that there was a special
and very important directors' meeting called
at once) he scurried out again upon the street,
his papers in his hat, and did the business
of the day on 'change. And then he went
back to the bank, and asked if Mr. Harleston
Bowdoin had got there yet.

Mr. Stanchion told him no. By that time
it was after eleven. But Mr. Bowdoin made
a rapid calculation of the distance (it never
would have occurred to him to take a hack;
carriages, in his view, were meant for women,
funerals, and disreputable merrymakers), and
hastened down to Salem Street.

Old Mrs. Hughson met him at the door,
grateful and tearful. Yes, young Mr. Harley
(she remembered him well in the old days,
and had been jealous of him as a rival of her
son) was upstairs. She feared poor McMurtagh was very ill. He had been out of his
head for days and days. To Mr. Bowdoin's
peppery query why the devil she had not sent
for him, Mrs. Hughson had nothing to say.
It had never occurred to her, perhaps, that
the well-being of such a quaint, dried-up old
chap as Jamie could be a matter of moment

to his wealthy employers whom she had never
known.

"Can I see him?" asked Mr. Bowdoin.
But as he spoke, Harley came down the stairs.

"It's heart-breaking," he said. "He thinks
he's in the South with her. He was going to
meet her, it seems; and the poor old fellow
does not know he has not gone."

"Let me see him," said the elder. "Have
they no nurse?"

"I nurse him off and on, nigh about all he
needs," answered Mrs. Hughson. "And then
there's John."

But Mr. Bowdoin had hurried up the stairs.
Jamie was lying with his eyes wide open, mov-
ing restlessly. It seemed a low fever; for his
face was pale; only the old ruddiness showed
unnaturally, like the mark of his old-country
lineage, left from bygone years of youth and
sunlight on his paling life. And Jamie's eyes
met Mr. Bowdoin's; he had been murmuring
rapidly, and there was a smile in them; but
this now he lost, though the eyes had in them
no look of recognition. He became silent as
his look touched Mr. Bowdoin's face and
glanced from it quickly, as do the looks of

delirious persons and young children. And then, as the old gentleman bent over him and touched his hand, " A thousand dollars yet! a thousand dollars yet!" many times repeating this in a low cry; and all his raving now was of money and rows of money, rows and rows of gold.

Mr. Bowdoin stood by him. Harley came to the door, and motioned to him to step outside. Jamie went on: " A year more! another year more!" Then, as Mr. Bowdoin again touched his hand, he stared, and Mr. Bowdoin started at the mention of his own name.

"See, Mr. Bowdoin! but one row more to fill! But one year more, but one year more!"

Mr. Bowdoin dropped his hand, and went hastily to the door, which he closed behind him.

"Harley, my boy, we must n't listen to the old man's ravings — and I must go back to the bank."

"He has never talked that way to me, sir: it 's all about Mercedes, and his going to her," and Harley opened the door, and both went in.

And sure enough, the old man's raving changed. "I must go to her. I must go to

her. I must go to her. I cannot help it, I
must go to her."

"Sometimes he thinks he has gone," whispered Harley. "Then he is quieter."

"What are these?" said Mr. Bowdoin,
kicking over a pile of newspapers on the floor.
"Why does he have New Orleans newspapers?"

The two men looked, and found one paper
folded more carefully, on the table; in this
they read the item telling of St. Clair's death.
They looked at one another.

"That is it, then," said Harley. "I wonder if he left her poor?"

"So she is not in Havana, after all," said
Mr. Bowdoin.

And old Jamie, who had been speaking
meaningless sentences, suddenly broke into his
old refrain : "*A thousand dollars more!*"

"I must get to the bank," said the old
gentleman, "and stop that meeting."

"And *I* must go to *her!*" cried Harleston
Bowdoin.

The other grasped his hand. But Jamie's
spirit was far away, and thought that all these
things were done.

XII.

Old Mr. Bowdoin went back to his bank meeting, which he peremptorily postponed, bidding James his son to vote that way, and he would give him reasons afterward. Going home he linked his arm in his, and told him why he would not have that meeting, and the new bank formed, and all its assets and trusts counted, until James McMurtagh was well again, or not in this world to know. And that same night, Commander Harleston, still on sick leave, started by rail for New Orleans, with orders that would take him through the lines. They had doctors and a nurse now for poor old Jamie; but Mr. Bowdoin was convinced no drug could save his life and reason, — only Mercedes. He lay still in a fever, out of his mind; and the doctors dreaded that his heart might stop when his mind came to. That, at least, was the English of it; the doctors spoke in words of Greek and Latin.

James Bowdoin suggested to his father that they should open the chest, thereby exciting a most unwonted burst of ire. "I pry into poor Jamie's accounts while he's lost his mind

of grief about that girl!" (For also to him
Mercedes, now nigh to forty, was still a girl.)
"I would not stoop to doubt him, sir." Yet,
on the other hand, Mr. Bowdoin would probably have never condoned a theft, once discovered; and James Bowdoin wasted his time in
hinting they might make it good.

"Confound it, sir," said the father, "it's
the making it good to Jamie, not the making
it good to us, that counts, — don't you see?"

"You do suspect him, then?"

"Not a bit, — not one whit, sir!" cried the
father. "I know him better. And I hate a
low, suspicious habit of mind, sir, with all my
heart!"

"You once said, sir, years ago (do you remember?), that but one thing — love — could
make a man like Jamie go wrong."

"I said a lot of d—d fool things, sir, when
I was bringing you up, and the consequences
are evident." And Mr. Bowdoin slammed out
of the breakfast-room where this conversation
took place.

But no word came from Harleston, and the
old gentleman's temper grew more execrable
every day. Again the bank directors met,

and again at his request — this time avowedly on account of McMurtagh's illness — the reorganization and examination were postponed. And at last, the very day before the next meeting, there came a telegram from Harley in New York. It said this only : —

"Landed to-day. Arrive to-morrow morning. Found."

.   .   .   .

"Now why the deuce can't he say what he's found and who's with him?" complained old Mr. Bowdoin to his wife and son for the twentieth time, that next morning.

Breakfast was over, and they were waiting for Harley to arrive. Mrs. Bowdoin went on with her work in silence.

"And why the devil is the train so late? I must be at the bank at eleven. Do you suppose she's with him?"

"How is Jamie?" said Mrs. Bowdoin only in reply.

"Much the same. Do you think — do you think " —

"I am afraid so, James," said the old lady. "Harley would have said " —

"There he comes!" cried Mr. Bowdoin

from the window. Father and son ran to the
door, in the early spring morning, and saw a
carriage stop, and Harley step out of it, and
then — a little girl.

XIII.

The image of Mercedes she was; and the
old gentleman caught her up and kissed her.
He had a way with all children; and James
thought this little maid was just as he remembered her mother, that day, now so long gone,
on the old Long Wharf, when the sailing-
vessel came in from the harbor, — the day he
was engaged to marry his Abby. Old Mrs.
Bowdoin stood beside, rubbing her spectacles;
and then the old man set the child upon his
lap, and told her soon she should see her
grandfather. And the child began to prattle
to him in a good English that had yet a color
of something French or Spanish; and she wore
a black dress.

"But perhaps you have never heard of your
old grandfather?"

The child said that "mamma" had often
talked about him, and had said that some day

she should go to Boston to see him. "Grand-father Jamie," the child called him. "That was before mamma went away."

Mr. Bowdoin looked at the black dress, and then at Harleston; and Harleston nodded his head sadly.

"Well, Mercedes, we will go very soon. Is n't your name Mercedes?" said the old gentleman, seeing the little maid look surprised.

"My name is Sarah, but mamma called me Sadie," lisped the child.

Mr. Bowdoin and Harleston looked each at the other, and had the same thought. It was as if the mother, who had so darkened (or shall we, after all, say lightened?) Jamie's life, had given up her strange Spanish name in giving him back this child, and remembered but the homely "Sadie" he once had called her by. But by this time old lady Bowdoin had the little maid upon her lap, and James was dragging Harley away to tell his story. And old Mr. Bowdoin even broke his rule by taking an after-breakfast cigar, and puffed it furiously.

"I got to New Orleans by rail and river, as you know. There I inquired after St.

Clair, and had no difficulty in finding out about him. He had been a sort of captain of marines in an armed blockade-runner, and he was well known in New Orleans as a gambler, a slave-dealer " —

Mr. Bowdoin grunted.

— "almost what they call a thug. But he had not been killed instantly; he died in a city hospital."

"There is no doubt about his being dead?" queried Mr. Bowdoin anxiously.

"Not the slightest. I saw his grave. But, unhappily, Mercedes is dead, too."

"All is for the best," said Mr. Bowdoin philosophically. "Perhaps you'd have married her."

"Perhaps I should," said Commander Harley simply. "Well, I found her at the hospital where he had died, and she died too. This little girl was all she had left. I brought her back. As you see, she is like her mother, only gentler, and her mother brought her up to reverence old Jamie above all things on earth."

"It was time," said Mr. Bowdoin dryly.

"She told me St. Clair had got into trouble

in New York; and old Jamie had sent them some large sum, — over twenty thousand dollars."

Mr. Bowdoin started. "The child told you this?"

"No, the mother. I saw her before she died."

"Oh," said his grandfather. "You did not tell me that."

"I saw her before she died," said Harley firmly. "You must not think hardly of her; she was very changed." The tears were in Commander Harleston's eyes.

"I will not," said Mr. Bowdoin. "Over twenty thousand dollars, — dear me, dear me! And we have our directors' meeting to-day. Well, well. I am glad, at least, poor Jamie has his little girl again," and Mr. Bowdoin took his hat and prepared to go. "I only hope I'm too late. James, go on ahead. Harley, my boy, I'm afraid we know it all."

"Stop a minute," said Harley. "There was some one else at the hospital."

"Everybody seems to have been at the hospital," growled old Mr. Bowdoin petulantly. But he sat down wearily, wondering what he

should do; for he felt almost sure now of
what poor Jamie had done.

"The captain of the blockade-runner was
there, too. He was mortally wounded; and
it was from him that I learned most about
St. Clair and how he ended. He seemed to
be a Spaniard by birth, though he wore as a
brooch a small miniature of Andrew Jackson."

"Hang Andrew Jackson!" cried the old
gentleman. "What do I care about Andrew
Jackson?"

"That's what I asked him. And do you
know what he said? 'Why, he saved me
from hanging.'"

Mr. Bowdoin started.

"Before he died he told me of his life. He
had even been on a pirate, in old days. Once
he was captured, and tried in Boston; and,
for some kindness he had shown, old Presi-
dent Jackson reprieved him. Then he ran
away, and never dared come back. But he
left some money at a bank here, and a little
girl, his daughter."

"What was his name? Hang it, what was
his name?" shouted old Mr. Bowdoin, putting
on his hat.

" Soto, — Romolo Soto."

Mr. Bowdoin sank back in his chair again. " Why, that was the captain. Mercedes was the mate's child."

" No. The money was Soto's, and the child too. He told me he had only lately sent a detective here to try and trace the child."

" The sheriff's officer, by Jove ! " said Mr. Bowdoin. " But can you prove it? can you prove it ? " he cried.

" Mercedes had yellow hair, so had Soto. And he knew your name. And before he died he gave me papers."

Mr. Bowdoin jumped up, took the papers, and bolted into the street.

XIV.

His son James was sitting in the chair, with the other directors around him, when old Mr. Bowdoin reached the bank. There was a silence when he entered, and a sense of past discussion in the air. James Bowdoin rose.

" Keep the chair, James, keep the chair. I have a little business with the board."

" They were discussing, sir," replied James,

"the necessity of completing our work for the new organization. Is McMurtagh yet well enough to work?"

"No," said the father.

"What is your objection to proceeding without him?" asked Mr. Pinckney rather shortly.

"None whatever," coolly answered Mr. Bowdoin.

"None whatever? Why, you said you would not proceed while Mr. McMurtagh was ill."

"McMurtagh will never come back to the bank," said old Mr. Bowdoin gravely.

"Dear me, I hope he is not dead?"

"No, but he will retire; on a pension, of course. Then his granddaughter has quite a little fortune."

"His granddaughter — a fortune?"

"Certainly — Miss Sarah — McMurtagh," gasped Mr. Bowdoin. He could not say "St. Clair," and so her name was changed. "Something over twenty thousand dollars. I have come for it now."

The other directors looked at old Mr. Bowdoin for visual evidence of a failing mind.

"It 's in the safe there, in a box. Mr. Stanchion, please get down the old tin box marked 'James Bowdoin's Sons;' there are the papers. The child's other grandfather, one Romolo Soto, gave it me himself, in 1829. I myself had it put in this bank the next day. Here is the receipt: 'James Bowdoin's Sons, one chest said to contain Spanish gold. Amount not specified.' I 'll take it, if you please."

"The amount must be specified somewhere."

"The amount was duly entered on the books of James Bowdoin's Sons, Tom Pinckney; and their books are no business of yours, unless you doubt our credit. Would you like a written statement?" and Mr. Bowdoin puffed himself up and glared at his old friend.

"Here is the chest, sir," said Mr. Stanchion suavely. "Have you the key?"

"No, sir; Mr. McMurtagh has the key," and Mr. Bowdoin stalked from the office.

XV.

Then old Mr. Bowdoin, with the box under his arm, hurried down to Salem Street. Jamie

still lay there, unconscious of earthly things.
For many weeks, his spirit, like a tired bird,
had hovered between this world and the next,
uncertain where to alight.

For many weeks he had been, as we call it,
out of his head.   Harley had had time to go
to New Orleans and return, Mercedes and
Soto to die, and all these meetings about less
important things to happen at the bank; and
still old Jamie's body lay in the little house
in Salem Street, his mind far wandering.   But
in all his sixty years of gray life, up to
then, I doubt if his soul had been so happy.
Dare we even say it was less real?   Old Mr.
Bowdoin laid the chest beside the door, and
listened.

For Jamie was wandering with Mercedes
under sunny skies; and now, for many days,
his ravings had not been of money or of this
world's duty, but only of her.   It had been
so from about the time she must have died;
dare one suppose he knew it?   So his mind
was still with her.

The doctors, though, were very anxious for
his mind, still wandering.   If his body returned to life, they feared that his mind would

not. But the Bowdoins and little Sarah sat and watched there.

It came that morning, — it was late in May; so calmly that for some moments they did not notice it, — old Mr. Bowdoin and the little girl.

Jamie opened his eyes to look out on this world again so naturally that they did not see that he had waked; only he lay there, looking out of the window, and puzzling at a blossom that was on a tree below; for he remembered, when he had gone to sleep the night before, it was March weather, and the snow lay on the ground. The snow lay thick upon the ground as he was walking to the station. How could spring have come in a night? Where was — What world was this?

For his eyes traveled down the room to where, sitting at the foot of his bed to be the first to be seen by him, Jamie saw his little girl as he remembered her.

Mr. Bowdoin started as the look of seeing came back to Jamie's eyes. But the little girl, as she had been told to do, ran forward and took the old clerk's hand.

It was very quiet in the room. Old Mr.

Bowdoin dared not speak; he sat there rubbing his spectacles.

But old Jamie had looked up to her, and said only, "Mercedes!"

XVI.

Jamie did come back to the bank — once. It was on a day some weeks after this, when he was well. He had been well enough even for one more journey to New York; the Bowdoins did not thwart him. And Mercedes — Sadie — was at his home; so now he came to get possession of his ward's little fortune, to be duly invested in his name as trustee, in the stock of the Old Colony Bank. He came in one morning, and all the bookkeepers greeted him; and then he went into the safe, where he found the box as usual; for Mr. Bowdoin, knowing that he would come, had taken it back.

When he came out, the chest was under his arm; and he went to old Mr. Bowdoin, alone in his private room. "Here is the chest, sir, I must ask you to count it." And before Mr. Bowdoin could answer he had turned the lock, so the lid sprang open. There, almost filling the box, were rows of coin, shining rows of gold.

Old Mr. Bowdoin's eyes glistened. "Jamie, why should I count it?" he said gently. "It is yours now, and you alone can receipt for it, as Sarah's legal guardian."

"I would have ye ken, sir, that the firm o' James Bowdoin's Sons ha' duly performed their trust."

And old Mr. Bowdoin said no more, but counted the coins, one by one, to the full number the ledger showed.

He did not look at the other page. But Jamie was not one to tear a leaf from a ledger. No one ever looked at the old book again; but the honest entries stand there still upon the page. Only now there is another: "Restored in full, June 26, 1862."